JOSHUA 10

JOSHUA 10

The Reconciliation Trilogy

John Elgan

2019
Trumbull, Connecticut

This is a work of fiction. All of the characters, organizations, and events portrayed in this novella are either products of the author's imagination or are used fictitiously.

JOSHUA 10

www.johnelgan.com

Library of Congress Control Number: 2019919270

ISBN 978-1-7342430-1-7 (paperback)
ISBN 978-1-7342430-0-0 (ebook)

First Edition: December 2019

For Lori

Introduction

THE SEA WAS OUR MOTHER, the land brutal and inhospitable to life. On land, air stole moisture from the living cell, tore at its fragile, fluid membranes and disrupted the vital chemical processes within. Air offered neither support against gravity's crush nor a medium as capable as water for carrying the sensual vibrations of sound. Air broke DNA's genetic backbone and the promise of an inheritance to future generations. It would take life over three billion years to solve the air problem and cross the boundary from sea to land. Yet the exploration and colonization of land earned a lavish reward: the powerful energy source of direct sunlight, superabundant raw materials and, unlike the teeming waters left behind, no competition for those who were first. It would be another four hundred and fifty million years of trial, and mostly error, before the dawn of humanity.

Throughout history, every society has told origin stories. The supernatural stories with their angels and demons have long since been cast deep into private spaces, while the sciences of evolution and genetics are elevated to public attention. What if the truth lies in the murk between science and the supernatural? What if the answers to the questions: "Where are we from? And where are we going?" are the same.

Our origin story begins somewhere in the middle, with the humans, as we observe the individuals that breathe air and die in their race to cross a new boundary — that between Earth and space.

One

COLONEL BERNARD IVERSON FOCUSED his steel-blue eyes on one particular gauge among the hundreds winking back at him from the spacecraft's control panel.

The Capsule Communicator, or CapCom, who linked Earth to Iverson in deep space, beeped in. "Joshua 10, this is Houston. Less than one minute to solar flare."

"Okay, Houston," replied Iverson. "How are the GCRs?"

"Galactic cosmic rays max out in one minute plus thirty."

Iverson checked the panel, hopeful the tests performed on this mission would lead to protection against cosmic radiation — the energy-charged fragments of atoms that travel through space at nearly the speed of light, bombard our bodies, rip into our organs, and create molecular shrapnel, which tear apart our cells from the inside. A successful test would mean humans, and the animals and plants we depend on, could finally venture in safety beyond the natural magnetic field that surrounds and protects life on Earth. So far, so good, thought Iverson. "Houston, I read active system magnets at full deflection. Passive systems intact."

"We confirm. Radiation barriers look good, colonel."

Iverson scanned a digital display of numbers and graphs. "Katherine's math was correct. Particle trajectory models match the measured."

Katherine Iverson, proud mathematician, Ph.D., astronaut and flight director, stood tall among Earth's NASA Mission Control Team — a dozen flight controllers, mainly engineers who monitor the Joshua 10 spacecraft. Katherine smiled at the CapCom.

"He can cook me a steak when he returns home."

The CapCom relayed the message to Katherine's husband. "Joshua 10, the flight director says the colonel can cook a steak for her when he returns home."

Iverson grinned and adjusted a few knobs on the control panel. "Roger that, Houston."

CapCom beeped in. "Joshua 10, we are reading in excess of five-hundred."

"Houston, which external panel is showing the five-hundred?" asked Iverson. "That's low for outside radiation."

Mission Control's environmental engineer read from his computer. "Internal cabin radiation levels *were* at five-hundred but are now climbing exponentially."

Iverson double-checked his gauges. Nearly twenty years ago he joined the Astronaut Corps, and this would not be the first time a spacecraft's readings differed from Mission Control's.

CapCom beeped in. "Joshua 10, we read five-hundred and rising for internal cabin radiation."

Iverson's attention settled on a needle gauge. The needle pointed within a green-colored band, well left of emergency red. "Houston, I read normal, five-zero internal."

Martin Smits, mission manager representing the project's private stakeholders, a personified business suit and tie, marched into the Mission Control room. "What's going on?"

"Flight Control and Joshua 10 read differently for cabin radiation," replied an engineer.

Katherine leaned in close to the CapCom. "Has he checked redundant systems?"

CapCom beeped in. "Joshua 10, check redundant systems." Iverson spun his chair around and glided his hands across the instruments that surrounded him.

"Affirmative," replied Iverson. "I don't read anything. Wait . . . what the hell is that?"

CapCom beeped in. "Joshua 10, internal radiation at seven-fifty and rising."

Iverson looped through his mental checklists to find the one model that might explain the difference in the readings. "Houston, I've had a problem here. I'm shutting down the active barrier. Request direct access to the magnetic field power control."

There was palpable tension among the Mission Control team. An engineer cautioned Katherine. "If he shuts down the magnets, only the physical shield remains."

Katherine ran the numbers. "That won't be enough." And if her calculations were correct, then her husband may already have been exposed to a near-lethal dose of radiation.

Iverson opened a panel that read "Magnetic Field Manual Shutdown." He reached deep inside. On his shirtsleeve, he wore the Ladonscorp Industries logo: a dark-green, five-pointed star.

CapCom beeped in. "Joshua 10, you do not have access to power down the magnets."

"There's a breach somewhere . . . a gap in the field," replied Iverson. "If Flight Control's readings are correct, something disabled my detectors." A drop of blood floated past.

Iverson withdrew his hand from the panel and wiped blood from his nose — too much blood.

"I need access to the magnets. I think the shield has inverted and created a magnifying effect within the cabin. I have to power down the magnets, now."

A few engineers huddled around a computer terminal and debated while Katherine stood beside the CapCom. Martin hovered behind them.

"He may be right," said an engineer. "And if Joshua 10's instruments are damaged —"

"Internal cabin radiation levels have exceeded detection limits," shouted the environmental engineer. Katherine's dark-skinned hand gripped his shoulder.

"Give him control."

Iverson rapidly adjusted knobs and flipped switches. His hands reddened. CapCom beeped in. "Joshua 10, you have full access to the magnetic field power control."

Iverson's lips blistered. He replied crisply despite excruciating pain. "Roger, Houston." He reached deep inside the manual shutdown panel and winced as he cranked the handle at the base.

CapCom beeped in, jubilant. "Joshua 10, we read internal radiation at normal. Levels below fifty: five-zero." In the background, cheers erupted from Mission Control.

Iverson withdrew his hand from inside the manual shutdown panel. His hand was raw muscle and bone; the skin sloughed off.

Two

ARTHUR DANIELS, LOOSE BONES IN A DARK SUIT, wriggled his way against office traffic through a corporate lobby past the Ladonscorp Industries logo and into an empty elevator. He was quick to press the Close Door button. A young mail clerk stepped in and spied Daniels's bony-finger dig at the button.

"Doesn't work," noted the clerk. "Not since the Americans with Disabilities Act. The doors have to stay open long enough for people with crutches or a wheelchair to get in."

Daniels placed his palm square on the clerk's chest and backed him off the elevator. "I don't see any crutches. And you don't want to need a wheelchair."

At the penthouse level, Daniels exited the elevator into a long, dark corridor and squeezed between immense carved doors. He was flanked on either side by gigantic wall-screens that arched over him in a room more cathedral nave than corporate office. The screens provided the room's only light — a montage of live images streaming from across Ladonscorp's vast global empire, from oil platforms in the frigid arctic sea to nuclear power stations along the steamy rivers of the Amazon. Ahead of him, where one might expect to find an altar, a white-haired man, his back to Daniels, sat in a leather throne of a chair behind an enormous desk of critically endangered Brazilian rosewood. Daniels crept forward.

"Excuse me, Mr. Typheus. The contractors claim that Ladonscorp pushed them too far, too fast. That our 'inadequate pretesting' of the radiation barriers led to the malfunction."

No response.

Daniels stepped closer. A drilling rig reflected on his face and added an industrial pattern to his suit.

"It's not public, sir. I'll take care of it. But we can expect a delay of —"

Typheus swiveled around to face Daniels. He cut an evil, laconic yet pompous figure in his mid-seventies. Everything was big about the man, except his body. Typheus spoke in a low voice. "The *first* to solve the radiation problem will dominate deep space travel. Fast-track Project Osiris."

"Mr. Typheus, Project Osiris has been on hold since chimpanzees became endangered. We'll need to apply for the research permits."

"Permits waste time and alert our competitors. No more delays."

"Any discovery will have to be legal for Ladonscorp to own it," Daniels argued. "After the Iverson incident, no primate facility *on Earth* is going to experiment without the required permits."

Typheus, silent and unmoved, stared right through him. Behind Daniels glowed a giant wall-screen image of a space station in orbit above the Moon.

Three

THE CLUMSY MOVEMENTS OF DONNY, an emergency worker in full hazmat suit, were tracked along a rubbled city street. On his sleeve, he wore the Ladonscorp Industries logo. Through his transparent face shield, a leashed border collie, Ted, was visible at his side. A remotely operated vehicle lagged behind Donny and Ted. It got hung up in the rubble that littered the otherwise desolate street. While the ROV's gears ground and its drivetrain whined, Donny and Ted forged ahead, climbing over the large and uneven obstacles.

Outside a small, mobile trailer, two military officers observed Donny and Ted through binoculars.

Inside the trailer, crouched over a computer screen and crammed with her technicians, Jessica Baris, Ph.D., directed Donny over radio. "Okay, Donny. Just you and Ted." Baris held a small device up to her microphone and pinched. "*Click Click*." She turned to one of her two technicians, short and chubby, Lou Pansotti. "Out of control. Reconnaissance drone is down. ROV is stuck again. So much for your machines taking over the world." Baris nodded to her other tech, tall and slim, Dr. Bud Schneider. "Project the virtual carrot."

Bud made a few rapid keystrokes. "Done. Head-up display activated."

"Okay, Donny. Find the target," commanded Baris. "Find the target. *Click Click*."

Through Donny's face shield, a bright yellow dump truck appeared in the distance at the base of a twisted lamp post.

The team tracked Donny and Ted on a live video display.

"The dog will get there first," said Lou.

Bud disagreed. "Donny. All the way."

"Wanna bet?"

The video display jumped and flickered. Slowly Baris turned. "I thought you guys fixed the damper."

"We did," they replied. "Or at least," Lou added, "I thought we did."

All business, Baris rolled her eyes. Delegate a task, she figured, and things will spiral out of control. "Not having this discussion. I'll do it myself." She turned her attention back to the screen. "Okay, Donny. Release, Ted. Release, Ted. *Click Click.*"

Untethered, Ted bounded off toward the lamp post. Donny scrambled after and trailed behind the dog.

"Once again, man's best friend proves to be the best," said Lou.

Ted veered off course and stopped to sniff the base of a fire hydrant.

"Hey, Bud," Lou whined. "That wasn't there yesterday."

"That's Dr. Hey, to you."

"Quit screwing around," Baris said with a glance at the officers outside the trailer. "We need this government contract, or we'll never get out from under Ladonscorp's thumb."

After years of toil under oppressive bosses, Baris had finally earned a project team of her own. Her unconventional work promised to fill the lucrative gap that remained between what humans and robots could accomplish in emergencies. Her decision to bring Donny's unique capabilities to the team made all the difference, but the attention he garnered had invited the intrusion of corporate micromanagers.

Lou pointed to the video screen. "Donny's starting to wander."

"Enrich the carrot," said Baris.

In Donny's transparent face shield, a bright yellow banana appeared next to the dump truck. Donny and the dog raced toward the lamp post. Bud and Lou stood and cheered at the video screen.

"Come on, Ted."

"Go, Donny."

Donny and Ted arrived at the lamp post in a photo finish.

"Winner," declared Lou.

"Certainly not. You imagined it," said Bud.

"Replay it. You'll see."

"No replays. Refocus, guys," insisted Baris through clenched teeth. "Donny is not out of the woods yet." Baris rubbed the tension out of her square jaw, and the team crowded the video screen.

Above the lamp post, the reconnaissance drone was entangled in a mess of overhead lines, which had been accidentally cut by its powerful rotors. On the ground below, no yellow dump truck or banana, Donny found only an artillery shell emblazoned with a biohazard warning.

Donny's gloved hands carefully grasped and lifted the lethal object. The rubble shifted beneath his feet, and the shell slipped from his hands toward the pavement. A moment before impact, Donny caught it.

A collective sigh of relief erupted from the team.

The overhead lines squealed and swayed. Below them, Donny unscrewed the warhead from the shell and removed a small cylinder marked "Danger. Do Not Handle."

Donny secured the cylinder within a small case attached to his belt and turned toward the distant command trailer to give a crooked thumbs-up. His radio crackled with Baris's voice. "Okay, Donny. Good work. Good work. *Click Click*. Bring it home."

Baris observed the officers outside nod their heads in approval. "Nailed it," exclaimed Baris.

"Uh, Dr. Baris," said Lou. "What's Donny doing?"

Baris turned to the screen. Donny was frantic. He heaved chunks of concrete far and wide as he dug into the pile of rubble.

"Donny. Bring it home. Bring it home. *Click Click*," called Baris.

Baris saw that Donny had caught the officers' attention. She opened the trailer door. Blinding sunlight and oven heat pressed inside. She jumped the steps to the parched desert floor and landed beside the officers. "Excuse me, gentlemen," she puffed through ginger locks that fell across her face. "Not a problem."

Baris hopped into a Jeep and raced away across a flat, desolate Southwestern landscape, beyond thickets of low shrubs and thorny bushes, to a mock-up of a bombed-out city block, the only hint of human presence other than a distant highway.

Baris was forced to stop at the large obstacles. She grabbed a backpack from the Jeep and scrambled over the rubble toward Donny, who continued to dig a hole and hurl debris.

"Donny stop. Stop," Baris demanded. *Click Click.*

Above Donny sizzled a frayed cable disturbed by his barrage of debris. Baris spotted the threat as the cable snaked out of the tangle of wires. She tackled Donny away from the cable, which thrashed across the ground in a shower of sparks.

Baris lay facing an impossibly blue sky and almost allowed herself a moment of reflection. Ted licked her face.

"They're leaving." Bud's voice called over the radio. "Dr. Baris, you need to get back here."

Baris rose and through binoculars saw the officers get in their car and drive off. Lou waved his arms to try and stop them.

Baris turned to Donny. "Shit. Bad. Very bad, Donny."

Donny sifted through the rubble in the hole he'd dug and lifted out a baby doll. The toy emitted a thin, mechanical cry as he cradled it against his chest and shuffled over to Baris. Next to her, he measured nearly two-feet shorter. Baris touched her forehead to Donny's face shield and then removed his hood.

Donny flashed Baris a wide, toothy grin. The display of his formidable canines belied the child-like affection he had for his trainer. Donny was an adolescent male chimpanzee.

With one hand, Baris gave Donny a banana from the backpack. "Good work. Good work, Donny." In the other, Baris pinched the training device. *Click Click*.

Baris returned to the trailer leaving Donny behind to navigate back with Ted. Beneath the blazing midday sun, the trailer shone bright, except for the Ladonscorp Industries name and logo; the large dark-green star, two of whose five points intruded upon the printed words, and purpose, of Baris's crew: Hazardous Environment Response Team.

Baris climbed to the roof of the trailer and adjusted the large telephoto lens of a camera aimed at the mock city. She discovered a loose piece at the base of the camera. She pulled a retractable pen from behind her ear, unscrewed it, removed the spring from inside, and jerry-rigged the repair. Through the lens, she observed Donny and Ted traverse a broad open plain on their way back to the trailer. A swirling updraft formed a small dust devil that briefly gave chase then destabilized in a dry wind.

Baris climbed down to greet Donny and shouted at the trailer. "Vibration damper is fixed, finally."

From inside the trailer, Bud and Lou enviously watched Baris lock in a warm embrace with Donny whom she had rescued from a Ladonscorp laboratory. They, too, had been saved by her — professionally and without affection. Bud was a blacklisted whistleblower and Lou the true and kind friend that stuck by him. Bud wondered aloud, "How can she be so hard and so soft at the same time?"

A cloud of dust gathered on the horizon and rolled toward the trailer. A black sedan appeared at the head of the cloud and snaked its way forward until it stopped a stone's throw away from Baris.

Baris stood ground, wary of the unexpected visitor. "Bud, settle Donny inside."

Bud poked his head out the trailer door and spotted the luxury sedan with its dark tinted windows. "Got it, Dr. Baris.

Okay, Donny." Bud pulled out a little yellow dump truck from behind his back. "Come inside." Donny grinned and ambled up and into the trailer.

"What about Ted?" asked Bud.

"Keep him close but loose," replied Baris.

Wind kicked up a cloud of dust that coiled around the car. Daniels emerged. His bony face and pale skin resembled the bleached bones that littered the desert.

"Dr. Baris?" The wind whipped up again and shook Daniels's blazer. He clutched his flapping jacket closed and hastened up to Baris.

"Dr. Baris, I presume?"

Baris regarded Daniels with suspicion. "Yes."

Daniels drew a folded letter from his breast pocket. "I'm Arthur Daniels, general counsel for Ladonscorp Industries. Let's speak inside."

"Actually, no." Experience had taught Baris not to act like an obedient pet unless you wanted to be treated like one. "We're a bit pressed for space . . . and time."

She plucked the letter from Daniels.

"You and your team need to report to the Ladonscorp facility in Kourou, French Guiana, tomorrow morning," said Daniels. "Private car service will pick you up at your home this evening at six. Separate arrangements were made for the rest of your team's transportation. Travel details are in that letter."

"Listen. Daniels, is it? Nobody is going anywhere. I had to reserve this training site a year in advance. I'm in charge of this site for one more week before we have to relocate. We're not leaving early to . . . I don't even know what for. What is this about?"

"You're familiar with the tragedy involving Bernie Iverson?"

"From the news," replied Baris.

"What you would not know from the news is that Iverson's mission was a Ladonscorp project — a very important Ladonscorp project."

"And this has to do with my work?" asked Baris.

"Your work is funded by Ladonscorp. A decision has been made to assign your team to the Joshua 10 project."

"But —"

"That is all I am at liberty to disclose to you."

"I'm sorry you had to come out this far for nothing," said Baris. "You should've called. Anyway, if you'll excuse me, we have work to finish here."

Baris turned back to the trailer and Daniels advanced toward her. Ted lept from the trailer doorway, barked at Daniels, then heeled to Baris.

Daniels froze and hissed after Baris. "Your work will be finished here — permanently."

Baris whipped around. "Excuse me? What do you mean?"

"I mean this is not a request," sneered Daniels. "Joshua 10 is the highest priority for Ladonscorp and its very influential stakeholders." Daniels strained a conciliatory tone. "Dr. Baris, if you can help get the project back on track, your team will have a bright future that includes your animals." He nodded toward Ted. Ted growled, and Daniels stepped back.

"The chimpanzee . . . Donny, is it? Once he matures, it's not easy to find work for an adult male — not outside a privately-funded medical laboratory."

Shoulders tight and raised, Baris glared at Daniels. "Why you . . ."

". . . understand how important your work and team are to you, Dr. Baris. A car will pick you up at six o'clock to make your flight."

Daniels turned, and Ted followed to nip at his trousers. "Ted, come," Baris called, then watched as the cloud of dirt wound its way back to the highway.

"Pack it up, guys! It looks like we're going on a trip."

Four

AT HOME, Baris organized a single suitcase atop her bed. Her husband, Tom Connelly, emerged from the bathroom and handed Baris a small case stuffed full of sundries.

"Why all the secrecy?" asked Tom.

"It's corporate. They play everything close to the vest." Baris dug through the case and tossed out all of the unnecessary items included by her husband.

"We hardly see you as it is. They can't expect you to drop everything and rush off to, to . . ."

"Kourou," said Baris.

"Where the hell is Kourou anyway?" asked Tom.

"French Guiana on the northeastern coast of South America, bounded by Brazil to the south and east, Suriname to the west, and the Atlantic Ocean to the northeast."

Tom raised an eyebrow.

"What?" said Baris. "I Googled it."

"How long will you be gone?"

"No return dates. I'll find out."

Tom shook his head. "Ladonscorp is going to owe us big time for this."

Baris hyper-organized the items in her suitcase. "That's for sure. The team has been preparing for rapid deployment. I just didn't expect this so soon."

"I meant us — your family," said Tom. "The job is consuming you."

"It's not 'a job.' It's my life."

"Wow. And me and Amanda? Where do we fit in?"

"That's not what I meant, Tom."

"Jessica, maybe we should consider —"

Amanda, six years old, scampered up a flight of stairs and into the room. "There's a big car outside!"

"We'll talk when I get back," Baris said to Tom, as she grabbed the suitcase. Tom scooped up their daughter.

The limo driver loaded Baris's bag into the car, and Amanda wedged herself beneath her mother's arms to hug her waist. "I love you, Mommy."

"I love you too, Sweetheart. Take care of your dad while I'm gone."

"Okay, Mommy."

"I'll miss you," said Tom.

Baris nodded and offered him a polite kiss. "I'll call you before takeoff."

The driver held the door for Baris. Tom and Amanda waved goodbye. Baris returned a final, uncertain smile.

Slumped in the back of the private car, Baris stared out the window at the guard rail streaking past. She didn't want to think about it; the words replayed in her mind, "It's not just a job. It's my life." A life of frequent moves. A life growing up in a new school every two years. She had earned her way to college and graduate school to gain some semblance of stability before . . . block that thought. Not something voluntary, it was a culture she was born into. And though she herself never served, she had adopted the military community's strong sense of duty. It's more than a job. Her work meant something. It carried responsibility, brought order to chaos, promoted safety, and conserved life. And then there was her team. Where would they be without her work? They depended on her. At least Amanda has two parents, she rationalized. She couldn't have been much older than Amanda is now when her own mother left her at her father's first Air Force change of station. Alone with her father, it was to his benign neglect that she credited her fierce independence and a grit born of necessity in the trade-off between having the freedom to explore the world and an unavailable caregiver.

"I've never picked you up before." The driver squinted at Baris in the rearview mirror. "First time?"

Baris was slow to respond. "Hmm?"

"How long have you been with Deinogen? I've been with them for over a year now. I drive all the execs and even some VIPs. Mostly pickups and drop-offs to the private airstrip." The driver passed a business card over his shoulder. "I also do work on the side. My number is on the back."

Baris stiffened in her seat. Nobody told her another company was involved in the project. "You don't work for Ladonscorp?" she asked.

"Deinogen. Science. Research. A lot of my clients were involved with that astronaut, Bernie Iverson. After his accident, I was swamped, long days, late nights."

"Your clients, business people? Corporate types?" asked Baris.

"Some. Mostly scientists. One of them was an astronaut and a genetic engineer. I asked him if he made those tomatoes that don't freeze. I cook a lot with tomatoes, especially —"

"So what did he say he did . . . the genetic engineer?"

"Mostly stuff that went over my head. Experiments with animals. Said his work could save astronauts from the kind of thing that happened to Iverson. Maybe I should have paid more attention in science class."

"Pull over," said Baris.

"What? Here?"

"Pull over. Now!"

The car pulled up onto the curb in the middle of a bridge and hugged the guard rail. Cars and trucks whizzed past dangerously close, rocking the limo, as Baris squeezed out and onto the narrow curb above a steep drop. She scanned the letter from Daniels and tapped away on her phone.

"I want to speak with Arthur Daniels. Dr. Jessica Baris."

Daniels stood at what might seem to be a respectable distance from Typheus, who reclined comfortably next to the phone. But it was fear that kept Daniels on the far side of the enormous desk. Daniels had to shout across at the phone. "Dr. Baris. Is the car late? It should have arrived at your home twenty-minutes ago."

Baris's voice echoed throughout the room. "Daniels, you are not going to fuck around with Donny or Ted. My team is under Ladonscorp, not Deinogen. No one is going to experiment with my animals. This trip is over."

"Who said anything about animal experiments? Who have you been talking to?"

"Never mind who I've been talking to. This ends now. I'll take my chances with corporate. I'll go outside if I have to."

"Listen, Baris. Where are you? You sound like you're in a wind tunnel."

"I'm on a bridge."

Daniels turned to Typheus and whispered. "Probably the driver."

"Problem?" asked Typheus.

"No. He wouldn't know anything. But I am going to need to give her something."

Typheus nodded.

Daniels slinked up close to the phone. "Dr. Baris, your team is needed to perform the tasks for which you have already trained. I assure you, there is no plan to conduct any experiments with *your* animals."

Daniels glanced at Typheus and continued. "After you and your team arrive at our aerospace facility in Kourou, you will be fully briefed on the details of your mission. Then you can decide whether or not your team will participate. Now, you have to catch that plane. It's a private flight with one other passenger. It must leave on time."

"No bullshit," demanded Baris.

"No . . . bullshit," replied Daniels. "Call me again if you must. Just make that flight."

Typheus tapped off the phone and Daniels retreated from the desk. "No 'experiments with your animals'?" said Typheus, turning his back to Daniels.

"Technically, sir, they're not *her* animals," said Daniels. "They are legally the property of Ladonscorp. If the government hadn't declared chimpanzees an endangered species, we could have used any one of the fifty other animals we used to have in our primate facility."

22

"In fact, we could still drop Baris," said Daniels, recalling his unpleasant meeting with her in the desert. "There are a few other animals not yet placed in a sanctuary, and her attachment to the chimp could be a problem. I think we should apply for the research permits."

Typheus swiveled around to face Daniels. "*You* think? Think about the narrow launch window. No more delays. No more discussion."

"Yes, sir," said Daniels, snapping to attention like a good little soldier.

"The package?" asked Typheus.

"The package is en route as we speak."

"And your two 'associates'?"

"Well placed," replied Daniels. He looked at his watch and sighed. "One of whom is about to begin what is likely to be a very long flight."

⊪⊶⊞⊶⊲Ⅱ

Baris boarded the private jet and surveyed the large, richly appointed cabin for a particular seat: a single seat, not a bench or club seat around a table; at the rear of the plane, preferably at an emergency exit, if there was one, which she could operate without depending on someone else; arguably the safest seat on the plane. She found it — already occupied.

"Excuse me. Would you mind if I sat there?" asked Baris. "I don't fly very well."

A weasel-faced man scrolled on his phone. "No humans fly very well." His attention remained focused on the screen. "I'm quite comfortable here. Thank you."

Baris squared off, and the flight attendant intervened. "Can I help you, Dr. Baris?"

Weaselface's ears perked up. Through narrow slits, his eyes followed Baris as the attendant steered her to the seat on the opposite side of the aisle.

"Here you are. Can I get you a drink?"

A cold look from Baris and the flight attendant disappeared down the aisle.

Weaselface leaned toward Baris who put on earphones to deny his presence.

"Flight attendant, prepare for takeoff," announced the pilot.

As the plane taxied out and accelerated down the runway, Baris, her life in someone else's hands, tensed and clutched the armrest. As the jet reached cruising altitude, Weaselface settled in his seat while Baris masked her agitation.

Weaselface received a low battery alert and plugged his phone into the charger beneath his seat. He unbuckled his belt and left to use the bathroom. In one casual movement, Baris stepped across the aisle, stomped the phone charger at the plug, and slipped back to her seat.

Weaselface returned and discovered his phone was not charging. He reached beneath his seat and felt the charger in pieces.

"You can use mine," offered Baris, politely.

Baris and Weaselface switched seats. Baris settled in her new seat while Weaselface masked his agitation.

⏵⏴⏵⏴⏴

The plane began to shudder, and Baris woke gripping the armrests.

"In just a few minutes," announced the pilot, "we will begin our descent into French Guiana."

Baris dared a peek out the window. Far below, stretching from west to east, a vast carpet of green equatorial forest met civilization's thin brown scar along the Atlantic coastline.

Five

THE JET TAXIED deep into a cavernous hangar. Baris was relieved to descend the stairs back onto terra firma. From out of the shadows, Bud and Lou rushed to greet her. Behind them, the Ladonscorp logo was splashed across the far wall.

"Am I glad to see you," said Bud. "I thought California's Hangar One was big. We had to ride back, just to see your reaction."

Baris's eyes darted about as she tried to penetrate the darkness. "Where are Donny and Ted? If they so much as harmed one hair on —"

"Don't worry, Dr. Baris. They're fine, just fine. They built a whole new state-of-the-art facility just for them," said Bud.

"Everything here looks and smells new," added Lou. "I've huffed so much fresh paint, even Bud looks good."

"Now you behave yourself," said Bud, then to Baris, "A veterinarian and two animal care workers are assigned. When we get back, I'll show you where they are."

A woman in a tidy business suit sprang from the shadows and stepped close to Baris. "I'll take you to see Donny and Ted. But first y' all need to attend a mandatory briefin' by the director. Please, Dr. Baris, this way to the car."

Weaselface passed unnoticed into the darkness.

⟋⟋⟊⟋⟊⟋⟋⟊

Baris and her team were tossed about the inside of the car as it sped along a deep forest road. They emerged from the forest into a broad clear-cut plain, and Bud and Lou shared a knowing glance. Lou lowered the window to provide Baris with an unobstructed view.

Baris was captivated. Outside in the distance, a majestic rocket ship punched a few hundred feet into the sky. The awe-inspiring rocket was attended by four lightning towers, each its own magnificent monument to human engineering.

"Centre Spatial Guyanais," announced the driver.

"The Guiana Space Center," Bud translated. "Europe and Russia assemble and launch rockets from here."

"Industrial chemicals and fuels," mused Baris. "Risk of fire, explosions, toxic vapors, and debris. They do need a hazardous response team."

"Lots of dangerous work for us down here," agreed Bud.

"Could be worse," said Lou.

"How do you figure that?" asked Baris.

"We could be going into space."

Everyone laughed.

Lou's shocked face. "We're going into space."

Baris, Bud, and Lou sat at a large table at the center of a fishbowl conference room. Visible outside the room was a mix of open office and technology workspaces. The Kourou launch director and lead astronaut trainer stood beside a screen, which displayed images of Earth-Moon orbit trajectories. The director briefed the accidental astronauts on their mission.

"We have only two weeks before the launch window closes. Your training will be abbreviated, enough to mitigate safety risks. Your mission aboard the space station will apply your —"

"The space station?" asked Bud.

"We're gonna orbit the Earth?" asked Lou.

"No," replied the director. "You are going into orbit around the Moon. It's called cislunar orbit."

"Why the moon?" asked Bud.

"For one thing, there's a lot less traffic," quipped the director.

Silence.

"Okay then," the director continued, "This mission, your mission, will pioneer emergency preparedness in space, aboard the Cislunar Space Station, or CSS."

Baris leaned in; the director had tapped into her sense of duty and piqued her curiosity. "The Joshua 10 program is an ambitious, *leading-edge* effort to achieve deep space travel on a scale unimaginable a decade ago."

"More like *bleeding* edge," Bud grumbled.

"Trailblazing does have its risks," said the director. "As we push farther into space, the orbital stations under construction and the bases on the Moon's surface will staff up with hundreds of people to mine for the mission-enabling resources that will be needed to supply outposts on Mars and beyond. Humans, robots, mining: high potential for accidents. That is why your expertly trained team, Dr. Baris — pioneering in its own right — will demonstrate that effective hazardous response is possible in deep space."

Baris shifted from interest to cautious enthusiasm. The director wrapped up the pitch.

"The mission crew will include the Mission Commander and a Systems Engineer, both of whom are already serving aboard the station. Your flight crew will include a Medical Officer and a Mission Specialist, three Payload Specialists — you folks here — and your animals. We are short the Mission Specialist. We need to fill that position before we can launch."

Weaselface oozed into the room. "Oh good," said the launch director, "Let me introduce your Medical Officer, Dr. Richard Caine." Richard displayed a crooked smile to the room.

Richard Caine was a physician, geneticist, and astronaut — quite the list of accomplishments for the youngest of eight raised in poverty without an emotional bond to either parent. At age seven he dissected the neighbor's cat, alive. When he was fifteen years old, he stole his teacher's phone and leaked her private photos. But perhaps that antisocial boy turned out fine after all.

The briefing concluded, and Richard approached Baris. He stared at her breasts. "Your work, Dr. Baris — it fascinates me."

Baris dipped her head to redirect Richard's smarmy eyes to her face. "You're familiar with my work?"

"*I* am the one responsible for your team joining the Joshua 10 project. Despite what others say of you, *I* know that you possess what the project needs to get back on track."

"And what exactly is that, Dick?

"It's Richard, please. I'm not sure how much you understand about space travel. The training, the launches, the conditions beyond the Earth's atmosphere — it's the most dangerous business, Jessica."

"It's Dr. Baris, please."

Richard fished for the information he needed. "Your team: two technicians, a dog, and what else? A chimpanzee?"

"Uh-huh."

"I suppose your technicians are responsible for the animals. You manage the technicians?"

Baris took the bait. "I train and command Donny and Ted. My technicians work the IT-end: computers, ROVs, training models."

"Oh," Richard grinned, "without you, Dr. Baris, there is no team."

⁊⊳⊲⊐⊳⊲⊏

Baris and her team entered another fishbowl conference room. This one exhibited various astronaut paraphernalia. The trainer led them over to a complete spacesuit.

"Although we do not expect you to spacewalk, you need to understand the basic functions of the EMU. In case of —"

"E-M-what?" Lou asked.

The trainer pointed to the spacesuit. "The Extravehicular Mobility Unit, or EMU," then pointing to its backpack, "and its Primary Life Support System, or PLSS." Baris's attention drifted, and she observed Richard on his phone outside the conference room. He was agitated, his voice inaudible.

Open office spaces are ill-suited to private scheming. Richard hunched in a corner of the hallway. "We're days into the training cycle. We need a Mission Specialist now.

Otherwise, the mission is a no-go." He listened for a moment. "Obviously," he whined. "Nobody wants to join a hasty civilian mission with animals. *I* told you so."

Richard glanced at Baris and her team. He continued in a low, desperate voice. "And Daniels, if I'm not aboard to retrieve the package, someone else will. You have to get someone, anyone."

Six

COLONEL IVERSON LAY IN BED and stared at the ceiling. ECG cables, I.V. tubes, and a ventilator connected Iverson's disfigured body to life support systems. He shifted his glance to Daniels, who hovered over him.

"That's why I'm here," pleaded Daniels. "Otherwise, I wouldn't ask you to do this. They lack experience and need someone they can turn to, someone to guide them. The crew needs a trained astronaut they can rely on to complete the mission and return *safely* to their families."

Daniels stooped to whisper into what remained of Iverson's ear. "Talk to her."

Iverson stared back at the ceiling. He considered Daniels's proposal and, in a sign of assent, blinked his eyes.

⚮⚮⚮

Baris, Bud, and Lou waited poolside wearing bright blue flight suits, helmets off. Richard stood behind the trainer prepared to assist. The trainer stepped forward and spoke with confidence. "Welcome to water recovery training. This exercise will prepare you for the return trip from your mission, should you have to make an emergency egress from the capsule."

Richard received a text message and stepped aside to view it. The screen read, "You have your final crew member."

The trainer continued. "If the capsule becomes submerged and you are disoriented, you must remain calm, certain that you can escape to safety. This exercise will help build that confidence." The trainer directed their attention to a pneumatic-powered sled at the edge of the pool. As the rest of the crew focused on their training, Richard snuck out of the room.

Richard quickly descended a stairwell and entered a room located below the pool. The door sign read "Pool Mechanical."

The trainer was buckled into the sled. Baris and her team peered into the deep water below. Lou fidgeted nervously, "Is it cold?" he asked.

"'Is it cold?'" said Bud, feigning courage. "What's the matter with you? There's nothing to be afraid of."

The trainer completed the demonstration, unbuckled the harness with ease, and stepped out of the sled. "The safety diver is in the pool to assist you. No worries." She scanned the doubtful faces of the crew. "So, who's first?"

Baris stepped forward, but Richard had returned to assist and maneuvered in between them. He placed a helmet on Bud's head, careful to keep himself between Bud and the others as he secured the helmet, helped seat Bud on the sled, and buckled the multiple-point restraint harness.

"Is there a problem?" asked the trainer as she strained to see what Richard was doing.

"No. There, I got it," replied Richard.

"Okay, Bud. Are you ready?" asked the trainer.

Bud gave a thumbs-up, and the trainer pressed a button. The sled plunged backward and turned Bud upside down beneath the water. Bud's fingers calmly located the harness buckle and depressed the release mechanism. It proved more difficult than he expected, and the buckle remained firmly locked. Then his helmet seal started to leak.

Bud panicked and yanked hard on the harness. The safety diver reached into the sled, pushed aside Bud's hands and attempted to free the harness. After he failed to unfasten the buckle, the diver pressed a large red lever to retract the sled from the water. Nothing happened.

His helmet full of water, Bud pressed his lips tight. His chin began to quiver as he desperately tried to hold his breath. He was terrified.

The safety diver erupted from the pool and shouted to the trainer. "Emergency switch isn't working."

Lou jumped into the pool without a helmet. He reached into the sled, wedged a hand beneath the harness straps to grab at Bud's motionless body, and placed his legs against the sled for leverage. He tried and failed to pull Bud's arm through the harness. A bubble formed from between Bud's lips — his final exhalation.

Lou's face turned purple, and he mustered all his strength to yank Bud's arm. With a muffled *snap* and *crack*, Lou wrenched Bud's arm beneath the harness strap, which enabled the safety diver to work Bud free and carry him to the surface.

Lou burst from the pool and coughed up a lungful of water. He saw Richard administering CPR to Bud and dragged himself over under the immense weight of his waterlogged flight suit. Baris knelt beside them.

Bud stirred and opened his eyes. Richard turned to Baris, "He's okay. He's okay." Baris stormed away to confront the trainer.

"What the hell happened?" Baris demanded.

The trainer ignored Baris and instructed the diver, "Let's replace the whole harness to be sure."

"Doesn't explain the backup failure. That will need to be addressed," added the diver.

Baris stepped between them and got up in the trainer's face. "You said, 'no worries,'" growled Baris. "You will be damned sure . . ."

Richard raised his eyebrows, and Lou smiled as they listened to Baris berate the trainer. ". . . test this shit of a contraption on yourselves before you even think of my team . . ."

Richard turned to Lou. "You dislocated his shoulder and elbow but saved his life. Nice job." Lou's smile twisted into a grimace, and he collapsed unconscious. Richard checked Lou's vitals and shouted, "Get the AED."

Baris and the trainer arrived at Lou's side with the defibrillator. Richard attached the electrodes to Lou's chest, and the AED powered up with a whine and a *beep*. Richard waved the others away. "Clear!"

Seven

THE SPACIOUS, BARE-WALLED INFIRMARY at the Kourou spaceport is equipped with six beds, but these are mostly temporary. Today, only one was occupied. Lou reclined in bed, and Bud lounged in a chair at his side wearing an arm brace. They relaxed alone in comfortable silence.

"Gentlemen." Baris's voice reverberated around the room, and the two grown men braced themselves for a good scolding. But Baris had a playful air about her, saying "Don't you two look comfortable?"

"No surprise I don't look too upset," said Lou, taking a long draw from a supersized milkshake.

Bud nodded in agreement. "Honestly, can't say I'm disappointed either," he mumbled through a mouthful of French fries, locally 'les frites.' "We are sorry, though; we can't be there with you." He offered Baris a fry.

"Thank you," said Baris, impressed with her techs ability to procure fast food anywhere in the world. "Only one more test to go. I'll be fine without you, boys. I hear the engineer on the space station is a real miracle worker."

Bud and Lou hung their heads, though Baris was quick to recover. "I mean you shouldn't worry about me. No one can replace you guys." She snatched up Lou's medical chart and read aloud the diagnosis. "Hypertrophic cardiomyopathy."

"Thickening of the heart," said Bud.

Lou smirked. "I'm thick all right. It's genetic."

"Now you behave yourself," snapped Bud with a hard stare.

"Okay, boys." Baris retreated from the room. "I can see you're back to your old selves."

Bud watched Baris disappear down the hallway. "You know, Lou, I'm still surprised at what happened in the pool."

"Things are moving fast," said Lou. "We're not *real* astronauts."

"Still, these facilities should have the highest inspection protocols. What's the probability of three defects at the same time?"

"What are you suggesting, Bud?"

"I don't know. Maybe the trainer should have fit my helmet. Even though Richard is an astronaut, he's the medical officer."

"You don't think Richard —"

"No."

"He saved both our lives," said Lou.

Bud nudged Lou. "You saved my life, partner. I just wish we could be there for Dr. B."

Baris was suspended off the ground, strapped into a metal chair ringed by what looked like enormous metal hula hoops. The whole machine rests atop a raised platform and might have been mistaken for an electric chair if not for the computer screen attached to one arm of the chair and swivels that suspend the chair inside the metal rings. This was the spatial disorientation simulator, or SDS.

Baris felt vulnerable. Richard lingered close to the simulator, and his proximity to her immobilized body made her more than a little anxious. It didn't help that the SDS Operator sat at the far end of the room, eyes fixed on the control panel.

The operator adjusted a microphone, and a speaker crackled to life above Baris. "Dr. Baris, after you complete your spin, continuous rotation in four axes of motion — planetary, pitch, roll and yaw, you will have ten seconds to complete the task displayed on your touchscreen."

Baris located the touchscreen attached to one of the armrests. Without looking at Baris, the operator continued. "I will now run the task on your screen so that you may practice before the disorientation test."

A simple set of instructions appeared on the screen, which required the selection of specific shapes in a particular sequence. Baris easily completed the task in only a few seconds.

"Very good, Dr. Baris." The operator's attention remained focused on the control panel. "Let me know when you are ready."

"I'm ready," shouted Baris, surprised at the adrenaline-pumped volume of her voice.

"Remember, Dr. Baris, you must complete the task within ten seconds to pass this test."

"Got it," replied Baris. *No pressure.*

The operator punched keys on the control panel, and Baris began to spin upside down and sideways through 360-degrees. Richard crept closer to the simulator, shifting his glance between Baris and the operator. The spin accelerated, and the start-stop feeling you get in an elevator relentlessly pulsed in waves throughout Baris's body — head-to-toe, toe-to-head, side to side. Repeat. Unfamiliar motion and a conflict between the orientation cues from her muscles, tendons, skin, eyes and the fluid in the canals of her ears sent a total mismatch of sensory signals to her brain. Baris wanted to vomit.

She tried to pick a spot to focus her attention and gain a sense of stability while the room swirled around her. Her hands, the touchscreen, the chair, the edge of the platform, and Richard — *rising toward her!* Baris's mind reeled with images of Bud in the pool, rescue breaths, chest compressions, Bud's eyes open, Richard fits the helmet.

The simulator slowed to a stop. Baris's head spun, and the room was a blur. "Dr. Baris," the operator's voice warbled. "I'm going to activate the task. You may begin now."

Baris's head was still spinning and her vision hazy. Her hand simply hovered above the touchscreen of blurred instructions.

"Five seconds remaining," announced the operator.

Rising nausea gripped Baris as she tried to focus on the screen. "I can't . . ." Richard's hand reached across and rapidly made selections on the screen. The operator looked up from the control panel as Richard stepped down from the platform.

"Dr. Baris," said the operator, peering over her glasses. Baris inhaled deeply. The operator slowly rose from her chair and walked toward Baris. "You have completed the task and final training exercise. Congratulations."

Baris shot Richard a quizzical look. He returned a saccharine smile. "Without you, Dr. Baris, there is no mission."

Eight

BARIS TOOK IN THE SCENE of the launch briefing room. Richard sat opposite her at the main table and pawed at something in his ear. Bud in a sling and Lou in a wheelchair sat off to the side and played the hand slap game — Lou's advantage. Not quite the "pioneering" mission she had been sold.

The launch director entered the room, leading a tall, confident woman. For Baris, their arrival lent a welcome air of credibility to the otherwise grade school atmosphere. "Let me introduce your Mission Specialist, Dr. Katherine Iverson."

Richard barged ahead and extended a sweaty hand. "Dr. Richard Caine, the medical officer on the mission. It is truly an honor to meet you, Dr. Iverson. And it will be a pleasure to work with you."

The director steered Katherine around Richard to Baris, "Dr. Jessica Baris, the research team lead."

"When I had a team." Baris shook Katherine's hand with a wink at Bud and Lou. "The walking wounded, Dr. Bud Schneider and Lou Pansotti." The two struggled to rise, and Katherine took pity.

"No need to get up, gentlemen. Thank you."

"After launch," said the director, "Dr. Schneider and Mr. Pansotti will join Space Station Mission Control in Houston." The director brought up a live display of radar and satellite images of the region around French Guiana. "Weather officers forecast favorable launch conditions. Let's review the countdown schedule for Joshua 10."

"I'm new to all this. Wouldn't we be Joshua 11?" asked Baris.

"Project names are normally serialized; however, only after success or accomplishment." The director made careless eye contact with Katherine and averted his eyes. "Your mission will be Joshua 10, designation HERO."

Lou interjected, "Hazardous Emergency Response in Orbit. H – E – R – O. Our idea." Lou went to high five Bud. Left hanging, Lou high-fived himself.

The Kourou animal housing facility was state-of-the-art. Robotic systems to empty soiled cages, a vacuum-assisted dumping station, tunnel-type cage washer, automated bedding dispensers, bottle fillers, and cleaners. It was almost too much for Baris to take in at once, at least when she first arrived two weeks earlier, and deliveries of new equipment had continued unabated even now as workers unpacked a large shipping crate in the room. Oddly, though, the only animals housed there had been Baris's. Ladonscorp recruited the young veterinarian in charge of the facility only days before Baris's arrival. She knew as much as Baris about the facility's history, which was nothing. The veterinarian, specialized as a space biologist, was apparently contracted for an obscene amount of money to acclimate a chimpanzee and dog for space travel under tight time constraints. She was to guarantee the animals' health and well-being from arrival to launch. The veterinarian had fulfilled her contract, and now just hours before launch, she watched Baris at play with one of her furry charges.

Donny gave Baris a banana — a gift. They hugged and gently stroked one another's hair. Baris made a point to visit three times daily: once when Donny woke, afternoon play, and at bedtime. Donny's body suddenly stiffened in her arms and Baris turned. Cheek to cheek, together they were transfixed by a gleaming metal cage weighing heavy atop a wooden pallet. The cage was constructed of galvanized wire mesh over a frame of steel tubing. Inside the cage was a false wall, which could be rotated and angled by a system of counterweights and pulleys. This internal wall, or squeeze-back panel, was designed to move in such a way that the animal inside is forced to come to the front of the cage and be completely immobilized. A tray was fixed beneath the cage and sloped to allow bodily fluids to drain into it. It was a crush-cage, used to facilitate the puncture of a vein to take blood samples, administer intravenous injections, or perform other procedures.

Baris hadn't seen such a device in years. Once commonly used in biomedical research, they had fallen out of favor because of the distress from fear it caused the animals. Not that the animal's emotions were valued, but a stressed animal released stress-response hormones, chemical signals inside the body, which introduced variables that might confound the outcome and validity of an experiment. Attempts to habituate animals to the cages: have them visit an empty cage, touch it, explore the outside; enter and exit freely without the trauma of the procedure that would eventually be performed; had all failed. Even the resignation that some of the animals displayed after prolonged restraint turned out to be only physical exhaustion. That was how Baris first found Donny's mother, depleted and in pain, as part of a new vaccine program to combat the latest filovirus outbreak. Baris believed there must be a better way, and her subsequent postdoctoral work in Ladonscorp's primate facilities helped confirm that chimpanzees could be trained to cooperate, rather than resist, and eliminate the behavioral and physiological distress. Now she was looking at a crush-cage sized for an adolescent male chimpanzee. The veterinarian quickly recognized the concerned look on her face.

"Not for my use, and not constructed for use in space," she assured Baris. "And certainly not part of the protocol for Donny. My job is finished here." Smiling, she added, "He and Ted have passed their final check-ups. It must be so exciting."

"I was completely against this project," said Baris, with a final, wary glance at the cage. "But this is once in a lifetime. Isn't it?"

"If it's any consolation, Donny and Ted have been thoroughly conditioned. They'll feel right at home aboard the station."

Baris gazed into Donny's calm eyes, and he offered her a sloppy kiss. "Ignorance is bliss," she said, and reached into Ted's kennel to give the border collie a good scratch under the collar. "See you in space."

It was a beautiful night for a space launch. From the windows of Launch Control, Bud gaped at the rocket remarkably balanced on the distant Launchpad: the pad pushing up on the rocket, gravity pulling it down. When the engines ignite, the thrust would unbalance the two opposing forces, and the rocket would rise and propel the Joshua 10 crew module into space. Bud glanced down at Lou's empty wheelchair, then at Lou who appeared at his side. "What?" said Lou. "I'm too nervous to sit." Behind them, the launch director and a row of flight controllers announced the progress of the countdown.

"One minute till launch."

"LOX up and down, 100 percent. Hydraulics power on."

"You are go for launch."

Perched atop the rocket and inside the crew module, Baris, Katherine, Richard, and Donny were strapped into their seats. Ted was harnessed in a deeply-cushioned crate. Katherine took a long, deep breath and exhaled, "An American crew on its way to an international space station, atop a Russian rocket, launched from a European spaceport, and funded by a private company. It's a special day when space crashes through barriers and erases borders for a better world."

Baris blanched, "Uh-huh," and tightened her grip on the armrests.

Richard noted Baris's anxiety and pointed to the unconscious Donny and Ted. "The vet should have hooked *you* up."

"And miss this?" eked Baris between shallow breaths.

The four main rocket engines rumbled on ignition, and the crew module rattled. Katherine was giddy in anticipation. "There they go. Four at a hundred."

"Guidance over to computer control."

"Thrust level at 100 percent."

Rocket engines roared.

"Here we go," bawled Richard.

"Uh-huh." Baris was grateful that flight suit gloves hide white knuckles.

Bud and Lou watched in awe as the rocket's fire and cloud lit up the sky like a titanic thunderstorm.

"Liftoff."

When the rocket reached space, the booster engines separated from the Joshua 10 modules, and the upper stage rockets ignited silently in the vacuum of space.

Richard smirked. "So, Baris, your first time. How was it?"

"It stinks."

Katherine nodded. "It can be unnerving at first, then you —"

"Yes. No, I mean it actually stinks. Does it always smell like this?" asked Baris.

"I smell it too," said Richard.

Katherine wrinkled her nose. "I got it now." She flipped a communication switch to reach the CapCom. "Kourou, we are detecting a strong odor — like urine."

"Roger that, Joshua 10."

Richard looked accusingly at Baris. Baris shook her head.

"Joshua 10, it is urine. Donny's in-suit biosensors are shorted out. His catheter must be leaking or disconnected."

The crew turned to Donny. He remained unconscious, drooling, and snoring. Baris rolled her eyes. *Ignorance is bliss.*

"Joshua 10, you're going to have to reconnect Donny's catheter. Be careful. Urine droplets could disable electronics and trigger the fire control system."

"Roger that, Kourou," replied Katherine.

Richard contemplated the fire detectors visible just inside the ventilation system along the module walls, and then he touched his nose with his index finger — no nose goes. "Not me."

"Oh, grow up," said Katherine, and turning to Baris, "I'm going to need your help, especially if he wakes up."

Baris surveyed the cramped cabin: three adult humans, an adolescent male chimpanzee, and a dog. *Oh my God.* "How many days until we reach the station?"

Nine

AFTER THREE DAYS into the trip from Earth to cislunar orbit, the crew module was a mess, cluttered with the accumulated debris you'd expect from three humans, a chimpanzee, and a dog.

CapCom Kourou beeped in. "Joshua 10, starting automated rendezvous with the CSS in near-rectilinear orbit."

Baris gazed out the cabin window. Against the lunar backdrop, the space station appeared small and insignificant. "We're all going to fit in there?"

Katherine placed her hand on Baris's shoulder. "It's still over a hundred miles away. Plenty of room."

The crew secured loose items to prepare for docking. Baris checked that Donny and Ted were buckled up. Richard observed Katherine suction the animals' urine from bags into the waste storage system and made the unusual offer of his assistance.

CapCom Kourou beeped in. "Final approach."

Baris peeked out the window. Outside, the station loomed large. The new Cislunar Space Station was colossal, comprised of dozens of modules, hubs, trusses, and expansive solar arrays. The central structure, large enough to reduce the effects of centrifugal acceleration, rotated to provide artificial gravity in the interior sections. When completed, the station would serve as part of a gateway to in-space manufacturing ventures and human-robotic technologies to extract and process resources from Earth's Moon, Mars, and beyond.

"Joshua 10, we are switching control from Launch Control Kourou over to NASA Space Station Mission Control Houston. Good luck."

The petals on Joshua 10's capture ring opened as it approached the station's docking ring. Magnets within the rings drew them together into a soft kiss.

CapCom Houston beeped in. "Joshua 10, this is Mission Control Houston. Capture confirmed."

"Roger that, Houston." Katherine was relieved to hear the familiar voice of NASA. The folks at the privately run Kourou Launch Facility were professional enough, but there's something about NASA's Houston Mission Control that inspired her confidence. After all, it was NASA's publicly-funded research and development that took on the initial risks and expense of acquiring new knowledge. Ladonscorp valued that knowledge only after they saw a profitable market.

CapCom beeped in. "Snap and hold closed. Hooks closed. Docking complete."

From the wide windows of the station's command module, two men monitored the Joshua 10 crew module as it attached to the docking compartment: Major Yuri Gladwell, the Station Mission Commander, hard-boiled soldier, lonesome cowboy; and Andy Faber, the Systems Engineer, affable Newfoundlander. The major shook his head. "Andy, go greet our visitors with their welcome patches and make sure the civvy doesn't break anything."

Two hatch doors opened between the station's docking compartment and the Joshua 10 crew module. Andy floated in from the docking compartment and assisted Katherine with the movement of the animals. "Welcome aboard the Cislunar Space Station," Andy said, placing a small patch on the hairless skin behind Katherine's ear. "Mind your step ahead as you transition from zero-g in the outer docking compartment to artificial gravity in the central modules."

Richard took off his wristwatch and fastened it to a seat, then maneuvered to ensure that he and Baris would be the last to exit. He reached the exit hatch just ahead of Baris and turned.

"Oh. Dr. Baris, I left my watch behind — on my seat. Would you?"

Baris turned back and located the watch. Richard squeezed urine from a bag directly into a fire control detector, slid the flattened bag into the vent, and floated out the hatchway into the docking compartment.

An alarm blared. "Fire control system activated," announced the station computer, as both hatch doors automatically closed and sealed tight, trapping Baris inside the Joshua 10 crew module.

Donny screamed and charged past Richard. He pulled wildly on the inner hatch to free Baris. Emotional memories of rattling cages and slamming doors fueled his rage; the trauma of a child separated from his mother. Trapped on the other side was Baris, and she was all he had known as comfort, joy, and safety.

Andy pushed Richard aside, reached the hatch doors holding a fire extinguisher, and maneuvered around Donny.

Inside the crew module, the ventilation system shut down, and the lights went out. Emergency lights flickered on and cast a dim red hue. Baris floated helpless and alone.

Andy manipulated the settings on a control panel beside the hatch while Donny continued to scream and pull on the doors. Richard peered through the hatch windows.

Inside the Joshua 10 crew module, Baris gasped for air. Richard implored Andy, "She's suffocating. Do something."

"I am doing everything," replied Andy.

The major arrived, floating past Katherine and Ted. "She's not suffocating. Panic attack. There are hours of breathable air."

Richard faced away from the crew, careful to mask his disappointment. "How long until you can get her out?" he asked.

Andy threw a switch. The alarm stopped. Donny let go.

"Now," said the major as he opened the hatch doors and withdrew. "Andy, I want a diagnostics report ASAP."

Andy ducked through the hatch into the crew module. Baris crouched alone; flushed, sweat-soaked, pathetic. Andy snuck her a sympathetic smile.

Ten

KATHERINE AND RICHARD SAT TOGETHER at one end of a table in the dining module. Baris brooded alone over her coffee with that all-too-familiar disconnected, new school feeling. Andy joined them.

"So, folks, that was a heck of a first day. A bit *alarming*, eh?"

No reaction from the sullen crew.

"Too soon? Okay."

Katherine tried to catch Baris's eye. "Donny and Ted seem settled in."

Baris nodded into her coffee, which had gone cold as she waited for the motion sickness meds to kick in. She massaged the transdermal patch behind her ear.

"Yeah. The AEM is a completely new design," added Andy. "No specs to work from. Engineered the animal enclosure module and wrote all the code, myself. Had to improvise. Real MacGyver stuff, ya know."

"The alarm, did you figure that out?" asked Richard.

"Urine set off the fire control system. Known problem. I told Mission Control months ago after SAFFIRE-seven. Even offered to redesign the —"

"Technology is only as reliable as the people operating it," the major said as he entered the dining module and glared at Baris.

"I handled the urine dumps," said Katherine.

"Respectfully, Dr. Iverson, you are a trained astronaut with flight experience. If this mission had been properly planned, you would not have found yourself in the unbecoming position of manually discharging animal urine."

"Perhaps if I had been more careful," said Katherine.

"I helped Katherine toward the end." Richard rose to leave. "If that was the cause, I'm just as responsible as she is." Then he ducked out of the module.

Andy tried to reduce the tension. "It's nothing personal. The major doesn't trust civilians or civilian missions. Major's military to the core."

"I completed the training," said Baris.

The major stood tall, arms to his sides as if called to attention. "Two weeks or two years? And before that, three years of related experience? A thousand-hours of jet pilot-in-command time?"

Baris's father had been a structural engineer in the Air Force, not a pilot, but she knew the major's type — high aggression, low agreeableness. She shifted to respond, but the major rolled on.

"Wiser men have said people believe that under pressure they will rise to the occasion, when in fact, they sink to the level of their training. What is your level of training, Dr. Baris?"

Before Baris could respond, the major turned his back on her to face Andy. "When you're done with this tea party, *Progress* needs unloading, and Joshua 10's ventilation system and FCS need rebooting. If you can't repair it, these folks can't return to Earth until we do. I doubt we'd survive the year."

Katherine watched the major as he marched out of the dining module, and her eyes grew wide. "We're marooned?"

"I'll fix it," Andy reassured her. "You can rely on Andy."

Richard quietly searched for "the package" among the containers on the Russian cargo ship, *Progress*. He located a cylinder the size of a large pencil case and slipped it into his pocket.

"Whadd'ya at?"

Richard jumped in surprise as Andy popped in at his side. Andy pointed to a single container stowed in the corner. "Med supplies are over there. Not many. We're a healthy lot."

Richard gathered up the few medical supply bags and slunk away.

Eleven

BARIS PACED BENEATH GROW LIGHTS, among the rows of hydroponic plants in the station's greenhouse module. She tracked Donny and Ted on a computer tablet, which showed the outline of the station's labyrinthine layout. Two moving dots tracked the remote location of Donny and Ted. Baris spoke into her headset.

"Okay, Donny. Good work. Good work. *Click Click.* Follow Ted. Follow Ted. *Click Click.*"

Katherine entered the greenhouse. "How's it going?" She gestured toward the tablet in Baris's hand.

"It's a challenge. No line of sight to track them. Just these quasi-static dots. There were supposed to be more cameras. I'll have to talk to Andy."

"You can rely on Andy," said Katherine, eliciting a slight turn in the corner of Baris's mouth.

"She does smile," said Katherine in mock surprise. "About the other day, the major was rough on you. You didn't deserve that."

"I get where he's coming from," said Baris. She had grown up in nearly half a dozen different places worldwide; neither right nor wrong, this was one more community that required adaptation to its peculiar way of doing things. She added, "I just need to prove myself."

Katherine turned to leave. "Don't hesitate to ask the advice of a military wife."

"How is he?" Baris called after Katherine.

Katherine circled back. "He's D.N.R. It's bad. Bernard always said, 'I expect a natural death from a spectacularly unnatural cause.'"

"Must be hard on you to be away from him."

"It's mostly the guilt."

"I can only imagine."

"Not in the way you might think," said Katherine. "There's nothing I could do for him. Here, I'm useful. I feel good for the first time in a long while."

⁂

Ted sniffed along the corridors of the station, each of the two-hundred million olfactory receptor neurons in his nose responding to the chemicals in the air. The human nose has less than six million receptors. Despite enormous investment in years of research, humans had yet to develop a technology as sensitive and discerning as a dog's nose. Donny trailed behind Ted as they passed the medical module.

Richard skulked in the doorway to medical and flashed a candy bar at Donny. "Hey, Buddy. Want this, don't you?"

Donny nodded vigorously, and Richard lured him into the medical module.

"Hop on up," Richard patted the seat of an examination chair. Donny followed the candy bar and climbed into the chair. The "package" cylinder recovered from the *Progress* cargo ship lay open and empty on the counter. Richard stuck Donny with an autoinjector syringe. Donny cried out.

⁂

Baris looked up and cocked her head. *Was that . . .?* Katherine leaned toward her, "What's your story? Is there a mister Dr. Jessica Baris?"

Baris considered Katherine's non-threatening demeanor. "There's a Connelly. We met in grad school. A whirlwind romance that ended in pregnancy. Not what I expected — not the plan." And not something she would typically share with someone she had only known professionally.

Katherine considered the training clicker in Baris's hand. "'Time and chance happeneth to them all.' You can't control everything, Jessica."

Baris averted her eyes toward the tablet. She noticed Donny had stopped at medical. "Donny. Donny, where's Ted? *Click Click.* Follow Ted. *Click Click.*"

Katherine could see Baris was distracted and uncomfortable with their conversation. "I'll let you go, Dr. Baris. I should get back to my own work." Katherine left, and Baris stared longingly after her. She couldn't recall the last time she opened up to anyone; without a home town, lifelong friends are hard to come by.

Inside the medical module, Donny rubbed the painful injection site. Baris's voice crackled from a small speaker fixed to his tracking collar. "Follow Ted. *Click Click.*" Donny drooled at the candy bar in Richard's hand.

"This?" Richard asked. Donny's face lit up with a broad grin. "This is mine. I'm not wasting it on a filthy ape." Richard took a big bite. "Go on. Get out."

Donny slouched out and knuckle-walked down the corridor to follow Ted.

Andy easily detached large panels of thick insulation blankets from the hull of the station, revealing a deep frame with hoses, ducts, and electrical conduit.

From just outside the docking compartment, Donny paused to study Andy through the hatchway as he detached and replaced the blankets. Andy sensed a presence and turned toward the hatch.

Donny was gone.

Ted returned first from the training run and exchanged a lick for a pat from Baris. Donny arrived a moment later, and he hugged Baris with an extra squeeze. Baris returned the affection — an uncomplicated relationship she could control.

"Okay. Good work. Good work, Donny. *Click Click*."

Twelve

THE CAPCOM BEEPED IN to the command module. "CSS, Houston. Over."

The major swiveled his chair over to the video screen. "Go ahead, Houston."

"Major, what's the status on repairs to the Joshua 10 module?"

The major flipped a comm switch to access an internal line on his headset. "Andy, Houston wants an update."

"System reboots didn't do the trick. I've had to dig a little deeper station-side to find the buggered settings," replied Andy.

"How deep?"

Inside the crew module at zero gravity, Andy scratched his head as he floated in a sea of parts he had disconnected from Joshua 10. "Mmm . . . Eliminated quite a few possibilities. I'll have it squared away soon."

The major rolled his eyes and translated Andy's report. "Houston. Initial system reboots failed. Ongoing attempt to isolate the tripped settings."

⁂

Alone in a silent corridor, Baris inclined against the hull wall and monitored Donny and Ted on the tablet. "That's odd."

"What's odd?" The major ducked in through a hatchway. He couldn't help notice how athletic Baris was, her back arched gracefully against the hull.

The major's wandering eyes were not lost on Baris. She pretended not to have noticed. "Over the past few weeks, Donny stops more often during the training runs," she said. "Then, somehow, he manages to make up the lost time."

"I don't understand," said the major.

"Well, I'm just a civilian." Baris chided him. "My explanation may be too simple for —"

"I get it. Look, I run a tight ship. Out here, there's no one to come to the rescue when something goes wrong."

"So *you* think I need to be rescued?"

"Okay. This isn't coming out right."

"You think?"

"Whatever the risks of your work, the folks back home believe it's important. Otherwise, they wouldn't have invested the resources of this station. And . . ."

"And?" Baris stood erect, expectant.

"Maybe I rushed to judgment. After all, you haven't broken anything in the month since you arrived."

"If that's the best you can do for an apology, then I accept."

"So *you* think I need to apologize?"

"But you just —"

"Carry on, Dr. Baris." The major did an about-face and marched down the corridor.

Baris and Katherine huddled over coffee in the dining module. Katherine was shaking her head. "'Carry on, Dr. Baris.' I can't believe he said that."

"Yep," smiled Baris.

"Someone has a crush on you, Jessica."

"Yeah, right. I'm a married woman."

"What happens in cislunar orbit, stays in cislunar —"

"Dr. Iverson!" exclaimed Baris.

Andy poked his head in the doorway and spotted Katherine and Baris blushing. "Has anybody seen my tools?"

"Which ones?" asked Katherine.

"All of them."

"All of them?" chuckled Baris, then turning to Katherine, "You can rely on Andy."

"Ha ha," Andy squawked. "It's not my fault it's taking so long. Just let me know if you find my tools."

"We will," Katherine giggled.

Andy exited. Baris and Katherine burst into laughter.

Thirteen

THE ANIMAL ENCLOSURE MODULE, or AEM, was constructed of transparent composite walls accessed through a keypad-coded locked door. Ted was kenneled, and Donny moved freely within the locked enclosure. Richard unlocked the door and entered. Ted growled at him, and Donny backed away.

"We started off on the wrong foot. Here, a peace offering." Richard tossed a candy bar to Donny.

Donny gobbled down the candy. Richard unwrapped another bar and drew nearer to Donny. In one hand, Richard held the offering of candy; in the other, gloved hand, he concealed an object behind his back.

Donny reached for the candy, grasped it, and brought it to his mouth. Richard grabbed hold of Donny's wrist and pressed the object against the bare skin of Donny's palm. Curious about the object in his hand, Donny didn't resist.

After a few seconds, Donny yanked back his hand and stared at his reddened palm. Ted barked wildly.

Hunched over his computer in the medical module, Richard recorded his data. "Exposed the subject's right hand to a radiation dose in excess of one-hundred gray. Tissue samples will be taken to assess cell damage and repair at twenty-four, forty-eight, and seventy-two hours, including DNA analysis." Richard turned to confirm he was still alone.

"It's been forty days since the administration of the viral vector. The injection site remains free of inflammation, and the subject shows no adverse reactions or side effects." He drained his coffee cup and switched off the microphone.

"One small prick for a chimpanzee; one giant payday for mankind."

ↂ⊳ↂ⊳ↂ

Daniels read the message on his phone and turned to Typheus. "It's from —"

"No names," Typheus interrupted. He waved Daniels aside as they stepped off the elevator into the dark and empty lobby of the Ladonscorp building.

Daniels heeled to Typheus. "It's been over a month with no side effects. Today, phase two is complete. If it works, we'll know within seventy-two hours."

ↂ⊳ↂ⊳ↂ

Inside the command module, Baris spoke with Bud and Lou over video link. "Has his overall time improved?" asked Bud.

"Yes," replied Baris. "Donny has been finding his way to the training targets faster, even though he's more distracted."

"How is that possible?" asked Bud.

Baris scrolled on her tablet. "I reviewed the training logs. The same logs I sent you. Donny stops more often, but he makes up the time. Somehow, he picks up Ted's trail without visual contact. Maybe he's following Ted's scent."

Lou shifted to the screen. "I originally thought Donny might be using scent. Bud says I'm crazy, but it seems like Donny predicts Ted's location."

"Predicts?" asked Baris.

Lou held a schematic diagram of the space station up to the video screen. It showed a black and white outline of the station to which Lou had added two colored lines. "Each line represents Donny and Ted. When Donny stops, he loses sight of Ted. Ted continues moving on toward the target. When Donny starts moving again, he takes a different path. Donny does not follow Ted's trail. He chooses the shortest route."

Baris replayed the latest training log on her tablet and traced Ted and Donny's route of travel with her fingers. They did take two different paths to the target location.

"Son of a . . . Lou's right," said Baris.

Bud returned on screen. "What does this mean, Dr. Baris?"

Baris stared at her tablet — at the line of Donny's impossible shortcut. "I have no idea."

"One more thing," added Bud. "Tom called me. Why is he asking *me* how you're doing?"

"I may have missed a call or two. I'll try and reach him next cycle. Thanks, guys. Good work." Baris cut the video link.

Fourteen

IN THE SERVICE MODULE, Katherine ran diagnostics on the station's acoustic dosimeters, which measured noise levels in the station. Outside in the vacuum of space, no one may be able to hear you scream, but inside the air-filled station, the omnipresent white noise produced by the station's compressors, fans, fluid pumps, and drives can lead to hearing loss, impair communication between crew members, cause headaches, and mask the subtle sounds that warn of equipment failures.

Katherine made a final inspection of the acoustic wiring inside a large cabinet. When she tried to close the cabinet door, something jammed it open. On the floor of the cabinet, the bag of Andy's tools blocked the door.

※※※※

Andy and Baris monitored Donny and Ted on Baris's tablet, which now included live video from Donny. Andy pointed a proud finger at the screen. "Not bad, wha? Added the camera to his tracking collar."

Images from Donny's point of view fluttered and jumped as he raced after Ted down the station's labyrinth of corridors.

"Fast bugger, isn't he. But have you ever considered organic robots?" asked Andy.

Baris pointed a proud finger at the screen. "Ever see a robot do that?"

Emergency strobe lights flashed throughout a tall, silo-shaped module located outside the edge of the central section of the station. Weightless, Donny scrambled up the inside wall, leapt across the module and swung from truss to truss as swiftly and surely as any wild chimpanzee in the forest. From far below at gravity's boundary, Ted barked up at the training target — a small canister placed to leak a trace of artificial smoke. Donny hung upside down, reached deep inside a control panel, and cranked a handle at the base. A heavy mist was released, which rapidly extinguished the smoking canister, and the strobe lights clicked off — training exercise complete.

Like humans, chimpanzees evolved a strong visuospatial orientation, and the organization of our nervous systems supported this perceptual temperament. Unlike humans, the more recent tree-dwelling origin of chimpanzees had pre-adapted Donny for the agile movements required to safely negotiate the structural chaos of a collapsed building or exploded power station. Now his evolutionary endowment bestowed breathtaking agility in the weightlessness of the outer modules — difficult for the humans, impossible for the dog — and perhaps even contributed to how little Donny was affected by the Coriolis effect in the rotating sections of the station. The human crew and canine were afflicted to various degrees with motion sickness, and Baris experienced it most when she traveled toward or away from the central axis of the station. In any case, Donny and Ted had performed their tasks well, and Baris was confident they could respond effectively to any emergency aboard a space station. The mission would be a success. She recorded her observations on the tablet.

"Donny seems to have learned his way around," said Baris. "That solves that one. Now on to the next mystery."

"Ah, the mystery," Andy nodded. "What mystery?"

"How Donny got that burn on his hand."

"I told you what I reported to the major. There are no exposed hot spots in this station — chemical, radiological, or thermal. Richard said allergies or stress could cause blisters."

"What the . . .?" Baris thrust the tablet at Andy. "We lost the video near medical."

Andy grabbed the tablet and frowned at the blank screen. "I'm on it. You can re —" Baris shot Andy a look, and he disappeared down the corridor.

※

Donny's gauze-bandaged hand fiddled with the camera on his collar as he entered the medical module. He rummaged through cabinets, opened and closed drawers, and peered into various apothecary jars.

※

Andy plodded along a corridor on his way to find Donny and stopped to catch his breath. "Sweet Mary Mother of God. This artificial gravity is killing me. Gotta' convince the major to let me slow down the rotation." Baris's voice crackled over Andy's radio. "I've got Ted. I'll meet you back at the mess."

"Roger that," replied Andy. "I've reached medical."

Andy entered the medical module and caught Donny covering a large jar. Donny furtively dropped an autoinjector cap to the floor and glared at Andy for a moment before his threatening expression dissolved into a playful grin. He ambled up to Andy; arms raised high.

As Andy led Donny out of medical by the hand, the bandage on Donny's hand loosened and fell to the floor. "That was stupid of me. Did I hurt you?" Andy examined Donny's hand. No visible sign of injury. "Must be the other one." Andy examined Donny's other hand. There were no signs of injury anywhere.

⁑

Baris gathered with Katherine and the major over a steaming tray of 3D-printed pasta with fresh "basil" — microalgae grown in the hydroponics module and genetically engineered to produce the essential oils that give basil leaves their warm and sweet aroma. Andy sauntered into the dining module, plopped into a chair, and shoveled a huge forkful of the pasta into his mouth.

"I'm no doctor," Andy croaked with a mouthful of food. "But Donny's hands look fine."

"I'm no Systems Engineer," said Katherine. "But these tools look like yours." Katherine slammed the bag of Andy's tools on the table.

"She saved your ass," said the major.

Andy reached for another scoop of pasta, and Baris grabbed his wrist. "What do you mean, *fine*? Donny's skin is full of blisters."

"Not anymore," said Andy.

Baris shot out of her seat and left the module.

Skeptical looks from Katherine and the major. "What," said Andy, claiming Baris's food tray, "nobody trusts Andy?"

Baris squatted inside the animal enclosure and examined Donny's hands. No blisters. No scarring. No evidence there had ever been an injury.

Baris stormed into the medical module. "Richard! Richard?"

The module was empty, and Baris decided to snoop around. There was a microscope, next to which lay a box of glass slides labeled: "Joshua 10 Project Osiris." Baris examined one of the slides under the microscope. "This was taken today."

Baris investigated further and discovered another set of microscope slides next to Richard's computer. Her hand disturbed the computer as she picked up the slides. The screen lit up.

Katherine and the major suffered the experience of Andy licking the last bit of sauce from the tray. "Can you blame us, Andy?" said the major.

"Doctor Iverson?" Andy pleaded. "You'd know."

"I'm not a medical doctor. Sorry."

"No need to take my word for it," said Andy. "Come and see for yourselves."

As they prepared to leave, Richard arrived in a hurry and punched up a coffee. The major pulled Richard aside. "When was the last time you examined Donny?"

"I need to get back to my work, Major." Richard had to wait for his cup to fill. "This morning. Why?"

"Andy claims witness to a miracle. Got Baris all excited." Richard tensed up. "Where is she?"

"Just left," said the major. "I thought to find you."

Baris searched for "Project Osiris" and "Joshua 10" on Richard's computer. No hits. She scrolled through the myriad folders on the computer: "Curriculum Vitae," "Grant Proposals," "Hologram Anime"?

It would take hours to navigate all of these folders, even if she knew what she was looking for. "I have to think like Richard." Baris paged down and stopped. "Of course." She opened the folder, "Nobel Prize."

Experiment Protocol CSS J10

Tissue Data Baseline

Tissue Data 24 Hours

Tissue Data 48 Hours

Baris typed.

> Copy Files over Quantum Line.
>
> To: Schneider, Bud; Pansotti, Lou
>
> Deliver to Pathology for analysis.
>
> Results to me ASAP.
>
> Reply over private comm link.
>
> My eyes only.

Baris could feel Richard's eyes bore into the back of her head. She whirled around and played offense. "You have a separate research entry for Joshua 10. Why?"

Richard simply stared at her. Baris stuck a finger in his face. "*You* are supposed to provide medical support for *my* work, *the* mission. I don't know what you're up to, but —"

"But nothing. What do you think you've found?"

"You're collecting tissue samples."

"Old samples. From work I —"

"These samples are fresh." Baris held up a glass slide.

Richard drew a long breath through flared nostrils and puffed out his chest. "*My* work will solve the radiation problem, prevent cancer, and reverse damage to the nervous system. *My* work will enable unlimited human travel beyond Earth's magnetosphere and permanent colonization of deep space."

Baris shook her head and pressed forward.

Richard backed away and his voice pitched high. "I can prevent the type of tragedy that Katherine has to deal with. My work will save lives."

"Where are those tissue samples from, Richard?"

"Your work? *The* mission. It's only a sideshow circus act. You don't get it. Cleaning up spills and putting out fires aboard a fireproof space station? Don't get in over your head, Jessica. You don't know what you're meddling in."

"One last time, Richard, where are they from?"

Richard considered his options. He was two hundred thousand miles from Earth and nowhere to hide from an enraged Baris. The execs at Ladonscorp would have to reign her in. He was not going down alone on this one. He spilled, "Project Osiris is —"

"Richard, are you in there. Over." The major's voice blared over the intercom.

"Yes. Go ahead, Major."

"Is Baris with you? There's something wrong with Donny."

Fifteen

BARIS AND RICHARD HURRIED to the animal enclosure. They found Andy, Katherine, and the major assembled outside the door. The major beckoned to Baris. "We came to check out Andy's story. And we saw this."

Donny was howling and bruising himself with his little yellow dump truck. Andy recorded the possessed behavior.

"I entered the mod first," explained Katherine. "He seemed fine and then all of a sudden he started seizing."

"I told everyone to back out," said the major. "We thought you and Richard should take the lead on this one."

Donny spotted Baris and froze. Baris unlocked the door, tread softly into the enclosure, and squatted to face Donny.

Donny gazed deeply into her eyes then exploded into frantic convulsions — flailing his arms and contorting his hands and fingers. Baris flinched but fought the impulse to flee in the wake of the fast and frenzied movements. Donny began to add a series of huffs, grunts, and growls; the flailing escalated to include his feet.

Baris spoke calmly. "Donny. Donny."

Donny froze. His eyes searched hers.

Baris spoke again, softly, as if to soothe a child. "It's okay, Donny. It's okay. I'm going to take care of you. *Click* —"

Donny lunged at Baris. A moment before impact, he stopped. Donny's breath stirred her hair. He stood up straight, hair bristling, shoulders hunched, and began to stamp his feet.

"I don't like this," said the major, and he turned to the crew for answers.

"I've got something to calm him," said Richard. "I'll be right back."

The major looked around for something that might serve as a weapon. "Andy, grab me that fire extinguisher."

Andy removed the extinguisher from the wall and handed him the heavy metal tank. Katherine cringed. "Is that such a good idea?"

"You have a better one?" asked the major.

In the medical module, Richard retrieved a vial from a cabinet and reached into the same jar that Andy had seen Donny holding earlier.

"Shit!" Richard jerked his hand out of the jar. A drop of blood welled up on his finger. Richard dumped the contents of the jar and discovered that among several autoinjectors, one of the syringes was missing its protective cap — needle exposed.

Donny, muscles stiff and tense, rocked side to side. He continued to hold Baris's gaze. Outside the enclosure, the major tightened his grip on the extinguisher and looked down the empty corridor for Richard.

"Okay. I'm not waiting any longer."

"We go on your count," said Andy as he reached for the door.

"Hold it." Katherine signaled Richard's arrival. "Richard, we were just about to . . ."

Richard stumbled toward them. Unable to speak, he pointed at Donny and collapsed. Donny relaxed and ambled away from Baris.

Donny held Richard's wide-eyed gaze as Baris and the crew carried him away.

⁊▷◁▥▷◁▯

Katherine comforted Baris over a cup of coffee. "Donny is under tremendous stress. He's in a new environment and suffered a painful injury."

"The way he looked at me, Katherine. Right through me. I've seen Donny respond to stress. If this is stress, then it's a completely new behavior for him." Baris sighed and slumped back in her chair. "I rescued Donny from a Ladonscorp research lab. I wonder if I made the right choice for him."

Andy and the major joined them at the table. "Richard is stable in medical," said the major. "Houston's flight surgeon said the effects of the drug he accidentally injected should wear off within a few hours, depending on the dose."

Baris leaned forward, "Major, I wanted to talk to you about something I found in —."

"Sorry, Baris," interrupted the major. "There's one more thing from the mission director. Your remaining training exercises are canceled. Your mission is over."

Baris sat dumbfounded. The major turned to Andy.

"When can we have the Joshua 10 crew module ready to take these two home?"

"Plus Donny and Ted," added Baris.

The major shook his head. "No. Mission director's call and I don't disagree with him."

Bud and Lou explored a long laboratory bench topped with a tangle of sophisticated equipment in NASA's new pathology lab. Bud marveled at the data graphically displayed on a large screen. "This is incredible."

"What does it mean?" asked Lou.

"That's the billion-dollar question," replied Dr. Jack Wryder, as he strode into the room waving a notebook. Tall, dark and handsome, he looked sharper in a lab coat than most men would in a bespoke suit. "The cells have been genetically modified: Chimpanzee DNA, herpes retroviral proteins, whole Tardigrade sequences, and genes from a bacterium, *Deinococcus radiodurans*. Where did you guys say you got this data?"

Bud and Lou exchanged a knowing glance and took a seat. Bud gestured for Jack Wryder to do the same. "It's a little complicated."

Sixteen

ALONE INSIDE THE COMMAND MODULE, Baris replayed Andy's video of Donny's bizarre behavior over and over again. Katherine entered and observed Baris, red-eyed, and glued to the screen. She placed a gentle hand on Baris's shoulder.

"I tried. Nothing is going to change their decision about Donny and Ted. They cite 'unacceptable risk.'"

Baris paused the video. Donny's image was frozen on the screen.

"Thanks for trying," said Baris. "I thought they might listen to one of their own."

Katherine stared at the screen; her attention fixed on Donny's image.

"What is it?" asked Baris.

"Again," asked Katherine.

Baris played the video and Donny resumed his wild contortions.

"Pause it," said Katherine. "It's sign language."

On-screen, Donny displayed signs with both hands and feet.

⊃⊱⊰⊱⊰⊲

Bud's skeptical expression filled the command module's video screen. "Sign language?"

"To confirm, we slowed the speed," said Katherine.

"Way down," added Baris. "He was signing so fast that at first it appeared to be random movement."

Lou poked his head on screen. "What did he have to say?"

"If anything, we can't figure it out," said Baris.

"I'm fluent in ASL and PSE," said Katherine. "Donny uses some of the signs, but altogether it's too complex."

"We tried, and failed, to teach Donny sign language for two years," said Bud.

"Yeah, there's a lot we're trying to make sense of. We sent you the video file. But first, what about Richard's data?" asked Baris, then aside to Katherine. "I'll have to fill you in."

"The cells," explained Bud, "were genetically engineered using a modified AAV-herpes hybrid as a vector to deliver foreign genes into the cells of the host. The files included the protocol for an experiment. Someone planned to inject a virus that will make the host resistant to radiation."

Lou popped in. "Dr. Baris, is this connected to Donny's behavior? Jack Wryder, the pathologist, said the host DNA was chimpanzee."

Baris bristled, "I'll kill the motherfu—"

Katherine cut the video link as the major entered the module. He found Baris and Katherine huddled over the blank comm screen. "What's going on in here? Where's Andy?"

Baris rose to leave. "He's repairing the crew module. And I'm going to tear Richard's head off."

"Whoa there, big guns," said the major, laughing.

Katherine stepped up to the major, "Seriously, you need to hear this." To Baris, "He has to know."

"Know what?" asked the major.

Donny knuckled up to the door of the animal enclosure and punched numbers on the keypad. The door unlocked.

⁘

Richard rested in the medical module, alone and paralyzed in the dark. At the sound of barefoot creeping, he opened his eyes. Cabinets clapped, drawers slid open and closed. There was the rattle of surgical instruments. Richard glanced sideways toward the noise.

All had quieted to the hum and whir of the fans gently circulating the air. Richard looked up and into Donny's eyes. Donny hung upside down directly above him.

Indigo stripes, like passing clouds, traveled across the skin of Donny's face.

Terrified, Richard struggled to move a muscle. He succeeded in twitching a finger.

Donny dropped.

⁘

The major had joined Baris and Katherine at the video screen. They watched Donny's contortions displayed in slow motion.

"I'm not buying the sign language," said the major. "The possibility of unauthorized experiments aboard my ship — now that really chaps my hide."

"Major," said Baris. "Whether you're satisfied or not, I'm leaving to kick his ass."

The major conceded. "We'll go together."

⁘

Andy listened to music on his earphones as he made repairs to the Joshua 10 crew module. In the adjacent docking compartment, Donny floated silent and unseen toward him.

Baris, Katherine, and the major entered medical, in the dark. Baris approached the examination chair while the major threw the light switch. Baris slipped on the floor, and Katherine caught her. The floor was slicked with fresh blood.

Richard's dissected corpse lay splayed out on the floor beside the chair.

Baris turned away from the body only to see bloody chimpanzee footprints crisscross the floor. The color drained from her face, and she leaned on the chair. "He's not capable of this."

"Did you lock the enclosure?" The major asked Baris.

"I thought I did."

Katherine stepped back from Richard's body to obtain a wider view. "Strange," she said. Baris and the major followed her curious gaze to the body. "It looks like an . . ."

"Angel," said Baris, mesmerized by the image. "A blood angel." Baris extended her arm and slowly waved it up and down. "Like when children play together in the snow and flap their arms and legs." Donny, she lamented, had no such semblance of a childhood. Removed from his mother to be raised by humans for vaccine development, Donny's birth had violated a moratorium on breeding chimpanzees. Ladonscorp was forced to place him in a sanctuary. But young Donny had not been properly socialized with his peers, which proved to be a problem when attempts were made to place him among the retired research animals. Donny appeared destined to languish in a Ladonscorp laboratory until her innovative work, so she thought, had offered Donny, and Ladonscorp, a way out.

Katherine knelt next to Richard's body, which had been partially dissected so that the skin from the arms and torso were peeled away into the shape of wings. "There's an awful lot of blood. Even if he was no longer paralyzed, he would have bled out before he hit the floor."

The absurdity of Katherine's suggestion had a sobering effect on Baris. "You think Donny moved him that way?" asked Baris. "Why would he do that?"

The major followed Donny's bloody footprints around the room. They trailed out of medical and down the corridor. "We're wasting time. He's headed to the crew module."

Baris and Katherine registered together, "Andy!"

⫇⧏⫇⧏⧉

Andy continued his repairs to the Joshua 10 crew module accompanied by tunes blaring through his headphones. Sensing a presence, he turned and jumped back. He accelerated in zero gravity, and his head banged against the hull. Baris reached out and grabbed hold of him. She removed his headphones. "Andy, are you all right?"

"I think I soiled my suit. You can't just sneak up like that."

"Have you seen Donny?"

"No." Andy rubbed the pain in the back of his head.

Baris turned to Katherine and the major who examined the area for signs of Donny. "Nothing in here," said Baris. "The blood trail ended in the docking compartment."

Andy floated up to Baris. "Blood trail, wha?"

"You better come with us," said Baris.

"Just one more adjustment, Dr. Baris. One more adjustment." Andy searched for something. "Where is it?"

Seventeen

"RICHARD'S DEAD." The major's somber face haunted Mission Control's giant wall screen. Bud and Lou gaped at the screen. The Mission Control Team: Director Henry Laughton, Manager Martin Smits, the CapCom, flight controllers, and several NASA scientists were all riveted to the screen as the major delivered his report from the command module.

"We believe . . . we know Donny is responsible."

Lou lunged in front of the screen. "Dr. Baris?" Bud hugged Lou away from the screen.

"Everyone's a bit shaken up but okay," replied the major, glancing over his shoulder at the crew assembled behind him. Baris sat apart. "I should've," she perseverated, "I should have put him in a sanctuary."

Henry, a bear of man, stepped up to the camera. "How did you contain Donny?"

"We didn't, Henry," replied the major. "We don't know where he is."

Now it was Bud that lunged at the screen. "You don't know where he is!"

"We're trying to activate Donny's tracking collar remotely. It's switched off between training sessions, but Andy may be able to activate it from here in the command module."

Henry lumbered up to the camera to look the major in the eyes. "Commander Gladwell, I want you to prep the Joshua 10 crew module for the immediate return of Doctors Baris and Iverson. Then —"

The lights flickered in the command module, and the video link with Mission Control was lost. The major turned from the blank screen and, together with Baris and Katherine, all eyes were on Andy.

"Wha?"

The voice of the station computer announced, "Module sixteen, starboard hatch closed. Manual interlock. Negative pressure. Habitat modules isolated."

"He c-closed a hatch," Andy faltered.

"Does somebody want to explain what just happened?" asked Baris.

"Donny closed the main hatchway," replied the major. "The one that connects the habitat modules — where we are — from the rest of the station."

"So we just open it up. Right?" asked Katherine.

"No. No. Not that simple." Andy squeezed his hands together. "There's negative pressure between the hatches. That automatically locks them closed."

The major read the crew's panicked faces. "We're good, all good. Andy, restore the comm link with Houston. Then prep Joshua 10 for return to Earth."

"I'm not leaving," Baris said to the major. "Donny and Ted are my responsibility."

"And you are mine, Dr. Baris."

"But I'm not leaving until —"

"Nobody's leaving," mumbled Andy.

"What was that?" asked the major.

"The repairs to Joshua 10 are not complete. When I reported the job was finished, I meant only a small adjustment was needed."

"Fine. Get it done."

"I can't. I don't have all the tools."

───✦───

Inside module sixteen, Donny turned a T-shaped tool on the starboard hatch to activate the pressure interlock. Satisfied, he ambled away, dragging the bag of Andy's tools behind him.

Eighteen

BARIS AND THE MAJOR consulted with Mission Control over the comm link restored by Andy. Martin scowled on screen.

"Major, you can understand why I'm having a difficult time believing everything in your report."

Baris leaned in to the microphone. "I discovered the tissue samples and forwarded Richard's files."

"Who is that, Major?

"Jessica Baris, sir."

"Oh, yes. Dr. Baris," Martin sneered. "The report also states that you failed to secure the enclosure, allowing that *monkey* to escape. Richard would be alive if not for your —"

"That report was only preliminary," interjected the major.

"Be that as it may," Martin pointed accusingly at the screen. "there is still . . ."

". . . a need to stay focused," added Henry. "One person is already dead. We need to ensure the safety of the remaining crew members, beginning with the status of repairs to Joshua 10. Commander, please?"

"One more task needs to be completed on the crew module," replied the major.

"Okay. What is your time estimate?" asked Henry.

Baris shouted over the major. "Well, that's just it. The major can't give you a time estimate."

The major swiveled around. "Hold on, Jess."

Baris pushed past the major. "What the major is too prudent to discuss is that the *chimpanzee* you refer to is an adolescent male that learned to operate a keypad to open his enclosure, kill a man who experimented on him, then close and lock a hatchway on a space station."

Lou whispered to Bud. "We've seen that face. They're in trouble."

Baris got right up into the camera. "Until someone has the balls to address the elephant in the room, we're not going to fix anything and sure as hell are not going to be able to ensure anyone's safety."

⊐⊐►◁⊐⊐►◁⊐⊏

Andy and Katherine searched for the tools throughout the docking compartment and the Joshua 10 crew module. Andy shrugged, "It's not that large an area. I know they were here."

"You lost them before," said Katherine. "I found them, remember."

"Yeah. Where did you find them?"

"Below the rack just outside the service module."

"Exactly. I didn't work anywhere near the service module."

⊐⊐►◁⊐⊐►◁⊐⊏

Inside the service module, Donny sat and pulled electronic components from the hull. He tossed the pieces onto a pile of hundreds of parts he had already cannibalized from the station.

Nineteen

HENRY CONVENED A SCIENCE TEAM comprised of Martin, Bud, Lou, Jack Wryder and a few of the NASA scientists. The team crowded around a small table set up in the rear of the Mission Control room. Martin opened with the cover story given him by his puppet masters.

"Ladonscorp Industries has released a statement. Dr. Richard Caine had expressed concern that funding would be cut for his work at their affiliate company, Deinogen. He had hoped the results from his *unauthorized* experiment would compel Ladonscorp to reconsider. Richard Caine acted alone."

"Why in space?" asked Bud.

"No laws to prohibit it," replied one of the scientists. "Unethical maybe —"

"But not illegal," Martin interjected.

Henry rapped his knuckles on the table. "We need to focus, work the data, keep communication open, and provide something useful to Major Gladwell and the crew. What do we know so far?"

"I asked pathologist Dr. Wryder to join us," said Bud, stepping aside. "He analyzed the data from Dr. Baris."

Martin wedged himself between Henry and Jack Wryder. "Those files are not public property. She had no right to involve an outside party."

"Privately-funded or not, Martin, I'm still the mission director. Let's stay constructive. There is no precedent for this situation, and we don't have enough information. The purpose of this team is to obtain actionable, scientific data."

Henry beckoned, "Dr. Wryder, what can you tell us? In English, please. Most of us here are engineers."

Jack Wryder dropped his notebook and a stack of papers on the table. "The methods used in the experiment, on the chimpanzee Donny, are identical to human gene therapy. Dr. Caine intended to make Donny resistant to radiation. If it worked, then it might also be used to make humans resistant to damage caused by space radiation."

"Did it work?" asked a scientist.

"The crew claim that Donny's injury healed completely within hours."

Martin could barely contain himself. "It worked!"

"Yes. And I believe the treatment is also responsible for Donny's recent behavior — accidental changes to genes that regulate brain function." Jack Wryder distributed a paper on these findings.

Everyone took a few minutes to read Jack Wryder's report. In part, he wrote that while a flu shot in a given year may contain up to four strains of a virus, this treatment involved a single injection with thirteen different strains. Each version of the virus was engineered to evade detection of the host's immune system and infect different types of cells throughout the body, inserting new genes that code for radiation resistance and repair functions. The infected cells manufactured and released copies of the viruses, which, in turn, went on to infect other cells until every cell with a nucleus had the new genes. The viral DNA also contained genes that enabled the infected cells to avoid detection by the body's defenses and inhibit the host's protective T-cells by over-stimulating their receptors. The injection had unleashed a massive assault on Donny's genome, and his body hadn't a clue what to do about it.

The latest gene-editing technologies, including a few novel ones, had been employed in the treatment to ensure the viruses would carry the new genes to specific sites in the host cell DNA where they could be inserted and expressed without harm to existing genes or known sequences that regulate gene expression. Wryder concluded, given the magnitude of this superinfection, it would have been impossible to control for the risks of harmful mutations and the recombination of viruses into new, dramatically different strains that could arise when the same cell is simultaneously infected by more than one virus. Thus far, he wrote, over one-thousand gene sequences known to be associated with intelligence had been collaterally disrupted by the treatment. The results might include: over-production of synapses, the communication connections between brain cells, particularly of the lateral frontal cortex and parietal lobe; higher metabolic rates, suggestive of more efficient neural circuits; and an increase in myelination associated with the white matter connectome and the transfer of information from one part of the brain to another.

One of the scientists tossed the paper on the table and crossed his arms. "My group used CRISPR and prime editing to precisely edit some of these same genes and observed nothing at all like this."

"Sure, you engineered what you targeted," replied Jack Wryder. "But with an understanding of less than twenty percent of your DNA, you don't know what the targets are or what they should be. Do you?"

Henry intervened. "What's your point, Dr. Wryder?"

"Richard Caine's experiment achieved its objective — complete radiation resistance — but with some *unintended* consequences."

Twenty

BUSY AT OPPOSITE ENDS OF THE COMMAND MODULE, Katherine and the major video conferenced with Houston while Andy and Baris worked to repair the tracking tablet. Andy turned over the tablet and snapped the cover closed.

"That should do it, Dr. Baris. Although, I'm not sure how much battery power remains in Donny's collar."

Baris turned on the tablet, and the quasi-static field dots blinked on the screen. "Donny's near the aft port of the service module," she said. "He's moving back and forth between the service module and the logistics module."

Andy reached for the nearest video terminal. "There's a camera in logistics. I can get us a visual."

The major and Katherine spoke with Henry over the video link. "We just got a fix on Donny," reported the major.

Henry's apprehension transcended his diminutive image on the small screen, and his voice blared in the command module. "Commander, the consensus opinion from the science team is that Donny has undergone extensive genetic modification and as yet unidentified neurological changes."

Andy and Baris observed Donny on live video. A varied collection of station components lay on the floor of the enormous and otherwise empty logistics module. Donny rummaged among the parts and seemed to select a few pieces at random. Then he assembled the pieces into a working device.

Andy and Baris gaped at the screen.

Henry continued the briefing. "Before you approach Donny again, we recommend looking for any unusual behaviors such as poor attention to tasks or difficulty concentrating, extremely watchful or "on guard" behavior, and —"

"Building things," Andy shouted from across the module.

The major turned to Andy. "What's that?"

Baris pointed to their screen. "Donny is building something."

"What's what, Commander?" asked Henry.

The major and Katherine abandoned the video link with Mission Control and joined Andy and Baris.

"My God. Is that normal?" asked Katherine.

"Not even close," replied Baris.

Henry faced a screen of an empty chair. "Where did he go?"

The crew observed Donny open a junction box and rearrange the circuit boards. Andy jumped back.

"No. No. No, Donny. Don't touch that."

"Electric power system override," announced the station computer. "SSU rerouted. Begin the habitat module shutdown sequence." The station's compressors, drives, fluid pumps, and fans whirred to a stop.

Complete silence. The mechanical sounds of the station were replaced with biological sounds, as each member of the crew became aware of the sound of their own breath, the pulse of each heartbeat, and skin shifting beneath clothes.

The major stretched to touch an overhead duct. "Ventilation system," his voice boomed in the silence. "It's shut down."

Andy whispered. "Lost electrolysis in the Oxygen Generation System and we're about to lose . . ."

Henry stared at the video link and watched the lights go out in the command module. The emergency lights flickered on, and the major's image darkened the screen. "Houston, there's a problem here."

Twenty-one

BARIS FLOATED WITH A MACHETE IN HER HAND — a menacing sight in the blood-red hue of the emergency lights. The major floated beside her in the Joshua 10 crew module. He squeezed the trigger on a stun gun, "Nothing."

"Taser with a dead battery and a machete," Baris scoffed. "This is the best the minds of NASA could come up with?"

"That's it from the landing survival kit," said the major, shaking out the Ortho-fabric rucksack. "If the Russians were here they'd have a gun."

"What about the *Progress* cargo ship?" asked Baris. "That's Russian."

"Automated. No crew rescue systems."

Baris turned the machete over in her hand. "I've got a better idea."

⌁⌁⌁

The major watched Baris destroy the blood-stained examination chair and bed. She hacked away with the machete until the long aluminum side rails fell clattering across the floor of the medical module. She gathered up the rails over to the counter where she dumped the jar of autoinjectors and opened a cabinet of drugs.

"Make yourself useful, Major, and fill up those syringes."

"How do we know these drugs will stop Donny," he asked. "Before he fights back?"

Baris wound medical adhesive tape around an autoinjector and the end of a bed rail. "We don't know. But neither does he. Use his intelligence against him. He knows what these might do."

Baris brandished a syringe-tipped spear. "Fear will be our weapon."

The crew assembled in the command module and Baris and the major distributed the spears among them. Andy weighed the heft of the shaft in his hand.

"Shit's about to get real, eh."

Katherine blanched at the screen displaying live video of the logistics module. "Guys, better take a look at this."

A large, complex, and sinister device filled the screen. Wide at the base, the device was tapered at the top and angled toward a window. Outside, the Earth was visible.

"Donny's been busy," said Katherine.

Andy pointed out features on the screen. "Those cables — there — are a direct feed from the station's main power supply. Whatever this device, it can suck the station dry."

"What about the solar panels?" suggested Baris.

"Too slow to recharge and power us through the next eclipse of the orbit."

The major corraled the crew. "We can't wait any longer. Andy, relay the live video feed to Mission Control and patch the comm link to our headsets. Baris take the lead with me, Donny's your boy. Let's move out."

The Mission Control team viewed the video playback of Donny building the device. From Donny's seemingly random activity emerged a sophisticated device.

"Henry, is that thing inside the logistics module?" asked one of the engineers as she consulted diagrams and made calculations.

"Yes, it is. Why?"

"It's aimed at the Earth."

Twenty-two

THE MAJOR AND BARIS led Andy and Katherine down several passages in the station. The major halted the crew at a closed hatchway. "Module sixteen."

"Okay, Andy." Katherine smiled. "Get us through."

Andy accessed a control panel and hot-wired the hatch.

Inside the logistics module, Donny crouched beside his device. "Module sixteen, positive pressure," announced the station computer. "Starboard hatch open."

Donny bolted upright.

Andy opened the hatches. "You can rely on Andy," he said, and allowed the others to pass first. On her way through, Katherine gave Andy a solid pat on the back.

The Mission Control team worked amid piles of empty coffee cups and take-out cartons. Henry stood to stretch his legs. "Okay, people. What have we got?"

An engineer wiped the fatigue from her eyes. "Apart from the individual components that were used to build the device, we don't know what they'll do in that configuration."

"And?" asked Henry.

"And that's about it."

"More," demanded Henry, and he gave the engineers a hard stare. It worked, and they ticked off a list of possibilities.

"Perhaps some sort of reverse kinetic inductance detector."

"Some of us think it looks like an electromagnetic pulse weapon capable of destroying electrical systems."

"Or it may not do anything."

Henry was losing patience. "We have to operate under the assumption that the device does something. Assuming that it can't do anything doesn't help us when it's powered up and fries our planet."

Henry pointed at an engineer. "You said it was aimed at the Earth."

"Lined up, really. Just a guess."

"For fu—," Henry's face reddened. "Folks, if guesses are all we have, then we need to move quickly from guesses to facts, and from facts to knowledge and wisdom."

⚗

Martin checked the bathroom stalls to confirm he was alone. He spoke quietly on the phone. "Your experiment worked. The chimp is radiation resistant. But there are unexpected side effects, which have become a much bigger problem. You don't understand what's happening here."

"I understand that you're paid to perform, not panic," replied Daniels. "The trail back to us ended with Richard's death."

"I fed them your story and covered for you. But the ape . . . what he's doing is unbelievable."

"We're interested in science, not science fiction. Don't call me, I'll call you."

⚗

A NASA scientist browsed Jack Wryder's notebook and quoted passages to the Mission Control team. "Donny's behavior is most likely an emergent property of innate genetic programming combined with an unimaginable increase in IQ. The instincts to build the device were already there, but unknown to human science."

"*Human* science?" jeered one of the engineers. "Is there any other kind?"

"Donny's new behaviors must be innate," the scientist continued to read, "like the complex behavior of beavers to construct dams or birds to build nests. Donny acts without conscious control."

"Okay, let's move on," said Henry.

"There's one more line. Wryder believes he found a matching DNA sequence in humans. 'It appears that approximately five million years ago, a common ancestor shared by chimpanzees and humans was genetically modified.'"

The scientist put down the notebook and looked up to find every form of incredulous expression from the people in the room. "Anyway, that's what Wryder speculates . . . in his notes."

Exasperated, Henry collapsed into his chair. "What Wryder speculates." Henry scanned the room. "Where is Dr. Wryder?"

"Jack left," Lou responded. "He said it was an emergency."

"And this isn't?" said Henry.

Bud pulled Lou aside, excited. "Five million years ago, Lou. Five . . . million . . . years." Lou returned a vacant stare and Bud grabbed him by the collar with both hands. "That's five million years before humans discovered genetic engineering."

"Wait a minute." Lou caught on. "How is that possible?"

"*I* don't know, Lou. But I think we both know someone who does."

⚇⚇⚇

In the dark of a windswept night, somewhere in the Gulf of Mexico, a helicopter touched down on a superyacht. Jack Wryder stepped off and on to the heaving deck.

Twenty-three

BARIS AND THE CREW reached a four-way intersection of corridors. Baris confirmed Donny's location on the tablet. "He's still in the logistics module."

The major halted the crew. "We're nearing the segment that leads to service and logistics. We can't allow Donny to circle around and cut us off from the habitat modules. We need to split up." He turned to Andy and Baris. "You guys will continue straight ahead and close the last hatchway leading to the service module." Andy nodded, and the major continued, "Katherine and I will go around and drive Donny away from logistics and toward you two. Then we'll close and lock the hatchway behind him."

"Trapping him *alive*," Baris confirmed, "in the corridor between module eighteen and the service module."

Andy stepped forward. "Then I can come back around, disconnect that device, and restore full power to the habitat modules."

"Sounds like a plan," said Katherine with a tap of her spear on the floor.

The major grasped the autoinjector at the end of his spear, "Remove the safety caps." And *pop* went the covers.

⅛·◁▯▷·Ⅲ

As Baris crept along the passageways with Andy, she noticed the dim red hue of the emergency lights cast long shadows along the hull — shadows deep enough to hide a predator from its prey. Baris wondered. Which are we, predator or prey? She shook the tablet. "Donny's tracking dot is gone."

Andy glanced at the blank tablet in Baris's hands. "Battery must have died. Our hatchway is just ahead."

Weapons raised and ready, they crouched toward the final hatchway between them and Donny's last known location. Baris recoiled. The tip of Andy's spear had grazed her shoulder, "Watch it with that." Andy lowered his weapon.

They neared the hatchway, which was barely visible at the end of the corridor. With every few steps they drew closer to Donny's last known position. Baris glanced at the blank tablet, hoping that Donny's signal would reappear and confirm his location.

They arrived at the open hatch without incident, and Andy inserted the shaft of his spear to jam it closed.

⟩⊲⊓⊳⊲⊓⟨

The major and Katherine prowled the corridors en route to the logistics module. Baris's voice crackled on their headsets. "We've secured the hatchway. Andy and I are going to go back around. See you guys in the logistics module. Be careful. We've lost Donny's signal."

"Roger that, Baris." replied the major, and he paused with Katherine before an open hatchway.

"Then what?" Katherine asked the major. "After we trap Donny."

The major signaled Katherine to mute her headset. "We cut off the section's environmental control and life support systems. He'll freeze to death before he suffocates."

"And Baris?"

The major searched Katherine's eyes for any sign of dissent. "We'll need some distraction until it's finished."

Katherine nodded her approval, and the major moved close beside her. "Donny can be anywhere up ahead. Don't let him slip between us."

Shoulder-to-shoulder, Katherine and the major cautiously stepped through the hatchway and resumed their sweep. Behind them in the hull wall, where he had listened as they conspired to kill him, Donny shifted beneath the insulation blankets.

The major and Katherine arrived at the entrance to the logistics module. They marveled in silence at the complex, towering device within. The major hand signaled Katherine to hold and keep watch as he entered the module alone. Confident that Donny lay ahead or in the logistics module, Katherine shifted her attention between logistics and the far corridor.

The major slowly stalked around the device and arrived back at the entrance. "Logistics is clear," he whispered and pointed down the corridor.

Katherine and the major brandished their spears and marched forward, shoulder to shoulder. "Final hatchway," mouthed the major.

Andy and Baris reached the location where Donny hid within the hull. The insulation blankets were loosened from the wall. Donny was gone.

As the major and Katherine closed the hatchway in front of them, soft footsteps fell from behind. Katherine spun around to face the threat, and her syringe plunged into the major's leg.

"It's only us," shouted Baris. Andy raised his arms in mock surrender.

Katherine inspected the major's leg and found the tip of the syringe had passed harmlessly in and out his pant leg. "Sorry?" she said, as the major grabbed her spear and wedged it in the gearbox handle to secure the hatch.

Baris peered through the hatch window. "He's in there?"

"Yeah," replied the major with a glance at Katherine. "He's in there."

Twenty-four

MISSION CONTROL BUZZED with activity. It was nearly an hour since their last communication with the crew trapped aboard the crippled station, and the Mission Control team had nothing to show for their efforts. Now, the situation was taking a turn for the worse.

"Station battery reserves are being drained."

"The device is powering up."

"Battery reserve dropping below ten percent."

Henry grabbed the comm link mic. "CSS, Houston. Over."

Baris and the crew entered the logistics module to examine the bewildering device. The major pulled Katherine aside. "When we return to the command module, you know what you have to do. Be discreet."

"CSS, Houston. Over." Henry's voice broke over the radio.

"Roger, Houston. This is Major Gladwell."

"You're losing power. The device is charging. You need to —"

The major shouted to Andy. "Disconnect it, now!"

Andy dove for the power cables.

The Mission Control team was roused to a fever pitch. Most of the flight controllers took to standing at their terminals.

"Battery reserve power at less than one percent."

"It fired! The device has fired!"

Henry furiously toggled the comm link switch. "CSS, Houston. Over. CSS, Houston. Major Gladwell, do you copy?"

"We've lost all communication," reported the CapCom. "I can't reestablish a link."

"Keep trying," demanded Henry. Then to an engineer, "How much time before the electromagnetic pulse reaches the Earth?"

"Five seconds . . ."

The room fell silent.

". . . ago." The engineer consulted a computer-generated graph. "No radiation detected across the entire electromagnetic spectrum."

"Woohoo!" Lou jumped to his feet. Bud pulled him down by the belt. "Sit down and behave yourself."

Martin strode up to Henry. "Nothing. It didn't do anything. I guess the ape is not as mysteriously intelligent as we . . . you thought."

⠿⧓⧓⧓

A tour guide gave a speech to a sleepy group of visitors at the Sanford Underground Research Facility in South Dakota. "For nearly half a century, we have been building larger and more sensitive detectors, yet dark matter keeps eluding us. For us to reach the sensitivity required to detect dark matter, the detector must be able to pick out only a few events per year. Without detectors of this enormous scale, the amount of time it would take to detect a signal . . . let's just say your grandchildren would be lucky to witness a signal."

The visitors shuffled into the monitoring room where a young scientist, feet up on a desk, passed the time with a Rubik's Cube. The tour guide paused in front of a giant wall-screen, which displayed live video of the detector itself — a deep, dark, underground fluid-filled silo. "A few years back," she droned on, "a single promising event was detected. Clearly, it's an incredibly rare event."

A modest chime rang out, and a tiny point of light glowed on the screen. The young scientist looked up. The tour guide halted the group. "It looks like a hit. What an incredible privilege it is to be here just when a particle signal is detected. Such an event is unlikely to occur again for years and years to come."

Another chime and a second point of light flashed on the screen.

"We are so very lucky today. Such an —" Another chime, and then another until the frequency of the signals escalated to a continuous ring. Billions of particles lit up the display until the full screen brightened up and washed out.

In complete darkness aboard the station, Baris brushed against the hull and flinched back. The hull was freezing. *Bop! Bop!* Someone tapped sharply on their headset.

"Comm link's down," reported the major.

"I can't see my hand in front of my face," said Katherine.

"At least we know where Donny is," added Baris.

An alarm blared throughout the station. "Catastrophic power loss," announced the station computer. "Critical systems shutdown. Environmental control shutdown. Life support shutdown."

The emergency lights flickered back on, and Baris was further apart from the crew than she had guessed by the volume of their voices in the dark. She edged up to Andy and asked, "How much time do we have?"

"Negative heat flux," Andy wiped away a layer of condensation forming on the seams of the hull. "Station's out of the sunlight and in the shade. We'll freeze to death before we run out of breathable air."

"We need to suit up." The major directed the crew. "Baris and I will head straight for the EMUs. Andy, you and Katherine reroute the power cables so that when we hit sunlight, the power flows to the habitat modules and Joshua 10. Then get into your EMUs. We're *all* going home."

⁊⊳⫸⊳⫷⫶

Inside the primary airlock, Baris and the major opened their personal lockers and dressed in their EMU suits. The major assisted Baris with her suit. "These will help control body temperature," he said.

Baris started to put on her helmet.

"No need for that," said the major. "For now, the station has breathable air. If you feel dizzy, or light-headed, it's time to put your helmet on. The suits will buy us enough time for Andy to make the final repair to Joshua 10, and then all of us can go home."

"You don't mean all of us. Do you?"

"I'm sorry, Jess. Ted will be fine in the AEM. But Donny," the major shook his head.

"No. I get it, Major."

"Jess, even if Donny hadn't . . . changed, without one of these EMUs, he can't survive."

Inside the logistics module, Andy and Katherine rerouted the power cables from the device. "That does it," proclaimed Andy, beaming with satisfaction.

Katherine waved a hand across the fog of her breath. "Not a minute too soon. It's getting chilly in here."

"Let's get to the EMUs," said Andy, and he stepped empty-handed toward the exit. Katherine stopped him cold with an arm across his chest. "Let's not forget the tools. I'd like to go home."

The Mission Control team video conferenced with a particle physicist from the Sanford Research Facility. Henry stared expectantly into the camera. "Dr. Randell, you say the particles you detected passed right through the Earth?"

"And every living organism on it," she replied.

Martin paced behind Henry. "And nothing was harmed? No damage in any way?"

"That is correct."

"You're sure?" Martin pressed her, concerned about the potential liability.

"We're sure of it," nodded the physicist.

"Then, no harm done." Martin relaxed and turned his back on the video screen. "The chimp got lucky and your research, Dr. Randell, gets funded for the next 20 years. That's it."

Dr. Randell twisted her mouth. "Not exactly."

Martin whipped around. "What do you mean, 'not exactly'?"

"My team believes that the device is a means of communication."

Henry rubbed his eyes in disbelief. Jack Wryder had offered wild notions of prehistoric genetic engineering, and now this. Henry was about to tell Dr. Randell an ape built the device but thought better of it.

Dr. Randall continued, "The device sent a single, powerful and patterned, burst of dark matter, which could be detected anywhere in our solar system and even as far away as distant galaxies." She bit her lip and squinted. "But there are no objects in our solar system in the line of sight of the device. And if the target is another galaxy, which galaxy? Or even which universe?"

"Which universe." Henry slumped back in his chair and swiveled away from the screen to face his team. "Come on, people! Anyone else?"

Twenty-five

ANDY AND KATHERINE reached the primary airlock and opened their lockers. Andy closed his locker and helped Katherine suit up. "Go on ahead, Dr. Iverson. I'll catch up."

"You'll catch up?" Katherine opened Andy's locker. "You don't have a suit. Where is your suit?"

An astronaut, in an ill-fitting spacesuit, ambled down a corridor. Through his helmet visor, Ted was visible at his side.

Baris helped prep the Joshua 10 crew module for departure. Each item she completed on the module return checklist brought her closer to feeling effective, confident, and in control. With a blip, Ted's tracking dot reappeared on her tablet. She double-checked the signal and spoke into her headset. "Major, I'm getting a signal from Ted's collar."

Inside the command module, Baris's voice crackled on the major's headset. ". . . signal . . . Ted's collar."

The major tapped his radio receiver. "Baris, say again. I'm not receiving."

"I'm going . . . him back to Josh . . ."

"Baris, I'm not reading you clearly. If you can hear me, don't go anywhere. Stay there. I'm on my way to you."

The major arrived in the docking compartment at the same time as Andy and Katherine. Andy shuffled along wrapped in an insulation panel. The bulk of the panel frustrated his attempts at a snug fit, and the excess material trailed behind him.

"Why aren't you suited up?" asked the major.

Andy shivered, and Katherine responded for him. "It wasn't in his locker. I was going to set him up inside Joshua 10 then search the other airlocks."

"F-first," Andy stammered to Katherine. "I need to walk you through the f-final repairs."

"Did you see Baris?" asked the major.

"Sounded like . . . she had Ted's signal," replied Andy. "The suit comm links are running weak beyond the distance of a f-few modules, but I'll go try and —"

Katherine touched Andy's arm. "You will stay right here and help me get us off this station."

"I told Baris to wait here," huffed the major.

"Even if she heard you," said Katherine. "Did you really believe she would listen?"

⌯⊳⟨⊳⟨⊳⟨⊩

Baris followed Ted's signal, which led her to a remote, unlit corridor of the station. She used the light of the tablet to illuminate her way forward until she heard sounds of clicking and scraping ahead in the darkness.

⌯⊳⟨⊳⟨⊳⟨⊩

The major tore through the animal enclosure module and found it empty. "Baris, how do you copy?" The major examined the kennel and door locks. "Baris, the enclosure was locked. Ted was let out. I think Donny escaped. Do you copy? Donny escaped."

Baris inched forward in the dark. She found Ted, panting in excitement and shrouded in the fog of his breath. She extended her hand to Ted, and as he began to step out of the mist, something yanked him back. Baris froze and held her breath. The fog reflected the light from her tablet, and she couldn't see where the leash led beyond his collar. The drum of her heart beat in her ears. She reached out slowly and followed Ted's leash.

The leash was tethered to the hull. *So where is Donny?* She referred back to the tablet and considered Ted's blinking dot. They were located at the far edge of the station, the farthest point from the Joshua 10 crew module. Baris knelt beside Ted. "Why all the way out here?" She ran a hand through his thick fur, lost in thought. "It's a trap."

The major discovered a trail of bright orange glow sticks, which, in the red hue of the emergency lights, cast an alluring sprinkle of vermilion, like embers from a campfire. "It's a . . ." Baris's voice scratched over his radio.

"Baris? I'm not receiving you. But I picked up your trail. It's beautiful. Hold where you are. I'm coming to you."

Baris released Ted. "Find Donny. Find Donny." Ted took off down the corridor and out of sight. The major's voice crackled over her radio. ". . . picked up your trail . . . to you."

Baris ran.

Indistinct, garbled voices hissed over the comm link inside the Joshua 10 crew module. Andy sleepily assisted Katherine in her repair work. "Reconnect tha-line to th-open . . ."

"To the open plug on the left side. Got it." Katherine observed Andy had stopped shivering. "You're hypothermic. Let's see if we can get you warmer." Katherine snuggled in close to Andy. She closed her eyes and took a deep breath. "Whew. Dizzy and my heart is racing. Do you have this effect on all women?"

"I wish. Put on your helmet."

"Promise I won't kiss you," she said.

"No, seriously. It's a symptom. Carbon dioxide levels . . . too high."

The major followed the trail of glow sticks through a hatchway and into a long, windowless corridor loaded with cargo containers emblazoned with the Ladonscorp logo. The walls were different from the other station modules. A thick fabric stretched over hinged segments of the module's metal frame. The major wound his way around stacks of cargo toward the open hatch at the opposite end of the module.

114

Midway in the module, hot sparks jumped from behind a stack of large containers. The major lay down his helmet and spear, and with long, labored breaths, he struggled to move aside the containers. Behind them, he discovered a bundle of severed cables. "Helmets on, everyone. Lines from the carbon dioxide scrubber are damaged." The major put on his helmet. "Baris, are you picking this up?"

Static.

"Andy? Katherine? Anyone, copy? Over."

Static.

The major picked up his spear and headed toward a faint orange glow coming from the hatchway at the far end of the module. The light ahead began to dim as the hatch doors started to close. The major quickened his pace around the jumble of containers and nearly tripped over something that brushed past his legs. It was Ted.

Ted leapt past and disappeared between the narrowing space in the hatchway. The major rushed forward and reached the hatch just as both doors closed and locked in front of him. He could hear muffled dog barks and then a *yelp*. He pressed his helmet to the double-hatch windows and strained to make out the shadows shifting beyond the hatchway. Donny faced the major.

The major pulled back from the window. Baris's voice blared inside his helmet. "Major, do you copy? Over."

"Copy that, Baris. You must be close. Donny is port side of the expandable."

"Major, it's a trap!"

The major tried and failed to force open the hatch. Donny's face vanished from the window.

On the other side of the hatch, Ted lay motionless with bloody bite marks on his paws and snout. Donny threw a switch.

Low mechanical moans were followed by creaking sounds above and below the major. The floor began to vibrate and heave. The major braced himself against the nearest container. Donny's face reappeared in the window. The walls wrinkled, and the port side of the module, where the major stood, separated from the station and began to contract like a giant accordion. Donny's image shrunk as a gap widened between the pair of closed hatches. Cargo containers tumbled and compressed as the module shortened. Impeded by the containers, the major battled his way back to escape through the hatch open on the starboard side of the module. Now that hatch began to close.

⁊▷◁▷◁▯

Baris raced to the major, navigating the twisted passageways with Ted's signal. She arrived at the expandable module as the hatch closed and locked ahead of her. She leaned up to the hatch window and cupped her hands for a better look.

The major was a few feet short of the hatch doors. Pinned away from the hatch between two large containers, the major reached for Baris. She tried to override the hatch lock. "I can't unlock it. How do I open it?"

"You can't," replied the major, now perversely carried toward the hatch.

Baris desperately struggled to open the hatch. "Hold on. Maybe I can pry it . . ."

"You can't, Jess. Turn away."

The shaft of Baris's weapon snapped as she tried to force the gearbox handle.

"Turn away, Jess." The major switched off his comm link.

Baris felt the major forced against the hatch. She stepped back and turned away. Inside the expandable module, the major was crushed. His helmet popped.

Baris might have cried — but she gasped for air, put on her helmet, and plotted a path to Ted's fading signal.

Twenty-six

HENRY STOMPED AMONG the members of the Mission Control team and cued up their status reports.

"Still no communication with the station," reported the CapCom.

"Engineering?" asked Henry.

"No signal that the crew module has left the station."

"Nevertheless," Henry flicked a finger at a naval officer. "The recovery teams will need to remain on alert. How about environmental?"

"ECLSS will have entered shutdown mode hours ago."

Henry massaged his brow. "Without the support systems, how long can they survive?"

"Not long," replied an engineer. She observed Bud and Lou's distress. "But the CO_2 scrubber does have its own emergency batteries. If they suited up, the EMUs could provide hours of breathable air — assuming they don't exert themselves."

Henry gave a hopeful nod and directed the CapCom. "Let me know the instant we have a comm link or signal from the crew module."

⚕

Inside the Joshua 10 crew module, Andy lay covered beneath a panel of insulation. Katherine knelt and placed a small canister next to him. "This is the only one I could find."

Baris returned, cradling Ted in her arms. Katherine observed a thick streak of blood — Ted's blood — smeared across Baris's eye and Ted's leg wrapped in gauze. "What happened to Ted?"

"Major's dead," said Baris, numbly.

Andy stirred.

"Donny is loose." Baris peeked beneath the insulation panel at Andy. "And he has your suit."

"The major? How?" asked Katherine.

"Trapped in the expan. . ." Baris trailed off into a far-away stare.

"We have to kill him," snarled Katherine. She dug around for something, anything, that might feel like a weapon.

"We have to leave," Baris said, gripping Katherine's arm. "We have to leave the station. Now."

Katherine buckled Andy into a seat and put the small canister in his lap. Baris harnessed Ted and peeled back the bandage to check his wound. "Your bleeding stopped." Baris ran her hand through his thick fur coat. "Hang in there, little bear." Baris gestured toward the canister on Andy's lap.

"Lithium hydroxide," said Katherine. "Removes carbon dioxide. We're getting him out of here just in time. Once we undock, Joshua 10's life support systems will kick in for the trip home."

"Home," Baris reflected. Images of Amanda and Tom brought an unexpected rush of heat to her chest. "Let's do this."

"Buckle up. I'll initiate the undocking sequence." Katherine flipped switches and checked gauges. "We'll be on our way in three, two, one —"

"Propulsion coupling error," announced the module computer. "Undocking sequence hold."

"Andy?" asked Katherine. "Andy, I'm going to need some help here."

Andy sat unresponsive.

"Andy!" shouted Baris.

Andy opened an eye.

"Coupling error," declared Katherine. "The undocking sequence is on hold."

"No problem," Andy responded dreamily. "Reset berthing switch."

Katherine scanned across the control panel. "I can't find the berthing switch."

"Not in here." Andy closed his eyes. "Out there."

⌐⊳◁⊐⊳◁⊐

Katherine glided through an airlock, released its EVA hatch door, and exited the station. Tethered to the station, she made a slow, steady spacewalk to the joint between the station and Joshua 10 crew module. "I'm there." Katherine located the switch. Beads of sweat from her face formed floating balls inside her helmet. "Resetting the switch to docking." Katherine smoothly rotated the switch. "Done here. Beginning my return."

"Roger that," replied Baris. "I'm keeping your seat cold."

Katherine smiled, not so much from the lame joke as from the fact that Baris made the attempt. She grasped along the station's handrails to pull herself back to the airlock. "At the EVA hatch. Entering the airlock in a few . . ." Katherine tugged on the hatch door. It didn't open. "Nothing's ever that easy." Katherine looked in the window at the empty airlock. She tried again and failed to open the hatch. "Jessica, I'm having trouble with the hatch."

"I'm on it," replied Baris.

Baris exited the crew module and found the hatchway leading to the station was closed. "Katherine, did you close the docking compartment hatch?"

"No."

"Well, it's closed now."

"That's not funny, Baris."

Baris warily approached the hatch. Donny's face flashed in the hatch window. "Shit!" Baris launched forward. The hatch was locked. "Katherine, I can't get to you. Find another EVA, fast!"

Katherine pulled herself over to the next hatchway. She glimpsed a spacesuit pass beneath the hatch. "Baris? Baris, where are you?"

"Docking . . . I . . ." The comm link weakened as Katherine moved farther from Baris. Katherine slid hand over hand to another hatch. It was locked. As she made her way passed windows to the next hatch, she spotted Donny inside moving slightly ahead of her.

Pulling hard on the handrails, Katherine launched herself far ahead of Donny. As she reached for the hatch, she was yanked backward before she could grab it. Katherine had reached the end of her tether. While she unclipped the tether and continued along the handrails, Donny reached the hatch before her.

Katherine was winded, and the balls of sweat inside her helmet had grown large enough to pose a choking hazard. "Baris?" Katherine wiggled down in her suit to avoid inhaling her sweat. "He keeps cutting me off."

Static.

"Baris?"

Baris braced herself next to the hatch door inside the docking compartment and swung a fire extinguisher against the wall. *Smash!* Katherine's voice, indistinct and garbled, crackled over the radio.

Katherine saw Donny on the other side of the hatch. He held her gaze for a moment and quickly broke away. "No you don't. You son of a bitch."

Katherine and Donny raced toward the last EVA hatch, which was located at the far end of the station and emblazoned with the Ladonscorp logo. Inside, Donny leapt on all four legs down the corridors. Outside, Katherine vaulted from rail to rail.

Katherine pulled ahead and flew toward the final hatch. Her hands grabbed the hatch, and her body swung over and past. She lost her grip.

Katherine floated away from the station. Two-hundred thousand miles distant, Bernard Iverson flatlined, and his soul departed to meet hers.

Twenty-seven

HENRY FIXED HIS EYES ON Mission Control's wall screen. An image of the space station pulsed red in its orbital path around the Moon. The CapCom reported, "DoD has a communications satellite we can use as a relay."

"How soon?" asked Henry.

"Line of sight in three minutes."

Speakerphone beeped in. "Director," announced the switchboard operator. "Call from Mr. Reeve Clark."

"Billionaire Reeve Clark?" exclaimed an engineer. "Founder of Digismoothie and SpaceMax?"

"Not now," Henry replied to the operator. "I'll get back to him." To the CapCom, "When we make contact with the station, prepare to —"

Operator beeped in. "Sorry, Director. He insists I tell you he can help with 'that thing going around that other thing that makes canines howl.'"

"How the hell does he already know?" said Henry.

"Director?" asked the operator.

"Put him through."

Reeve Clark basked in the moonlight, which cast deep shadows about the slippery deck of his superyacht, *JULIET*. He held a digismoothie in one hand and a satellite phone in the other. "Hello Henry," he said with a broad, canny grin.

"We're a little busy here, Reeve. Cut to it."

"I've retasked our spaceplane, *Kharon*, to fly by the cislunar space station."

Jack Wryder emerged, silent, from the shadows. Reeve continued, "Might even intercept it, Henry. If for some reason you'd like that to happen."

"You have my attention," said Henry.

⏃⫷⫶⫸⏄

Baris continued to slam the extinguisher against the wall until her effort produced a small breach. She squeezed her hand through and released the hatch. Alarm chimes blared inside her helmet. She checked her suit display: "low oxygen levels."

Baris returned to the Joshua 10 crew module for a quick check on Andy and Ted — both unresponsive. She rushed from airlock to airlock, and unlocking each EVA hatch, she poked her head outside the station to find Katherine. Out of breath and low on oxygen, she tried to control her breathing. "Katherine, do you copy? Over."

Static.

"Katherine, do you copy? Over."

Static.

"Goddammit, Katherine. You can't leave me here alone."

An indistinct voice crackled over the radio. Baris called out in hope, "Katherine!"

"CSS, this is Houston." It was the CapCom. "How do you read? Over."

Baris sank. "Tom. Oh, Tom."

All ears in the Mission Control room waited for another word, any word, from the station. "Over to you, sir." The CapCom turned the comm link over to Henry.

"CSS, who's speaking?"

"This is Baris."

"Baris, it's great to hear your voice," said Henry as joyful jabber erupted from Mission Control. Aside to the CapCom, "Can the whole station crew pick up our signal?"

The CapCom nodded, and Henry smiled. "Commander Gladwell, do you copy? Over."

"Major's dead," replied Baris.

Mission Control fell silent. An engineer reported to Henry in a low voice, "We're receiving the vital sign data. We read *two* suits, Dr. Baris and Andrew Faber."

"Shit." Henry shook his head and returned to the comm link. "I'm sorry, Baris. We read vitals for you and Andy."

Baris sat back against the hull in a remote airlock. Elbows on her knees, hands on either side of her helmet, she exhaled, "That's Donny. He's got Andy's suit."

"Baris, we're going to get you out of there. Where are you? We need you to get to the Joshua 10 crew module. Can you do that? Over."

Andy and Ted lay sprawled at Donny's feet as he listened, stiff and still, for Baris's reply. "Yeah. I can do that."

Baris began the long trudge back from the most remote airlock. With the station's mechanical systems down and the insulation panels acting as sound-absorbing baffles, there were no discernable sounds beyond the scratch of her breath and drub in her chest. Without auditory stimuli, her brain conjured up noises of its own, haunting Baris with enigmatic sounds on her way back to the crew module.

Twenty-eight

HENRY BOUNCED between the flight controllers. "We get only one shot at this," he rallied his team. "Where are we?"

"Her oxygen levels are near critical limits."

"Would she be better off without the suit?" asked Henry.

"CO_2 levels are over seven percent. She'd be unconscious before she secured the hatch."

"And the *Kharon*?" asked Henry.

"Spaceplane *Kharon* will be in range within five minutes."

Henry signaled the CapCom. "Get Baris on the comm."

Baris entered microgravity in the docking compartment and floated toward the Joshua 10 crew module. "Entering the docking compartment."

"Once you're inside," said Henry. "We'll step you through the —"

"Hatch is closed." Baris halted. "I left it open." The hair rose on the back of her neck. Donny seized her from behind, compressing her suit controls.

Henry bore down on the CapCom. "Baris? Baris, do you copy?"

The CapCom toggled the control switch. "Henry, her comm is switched off."

Baris struggled to reach the hatch to Joshua 10, but Donny restrained her. She fought like a wild animal to free herself while Donny calmly applied the powerful, steady grip of his arms and legs to hold her back. Baris flailed, and the alarm blared inside her helmet: "oxygen levels critical."

Baris gasped for air. Helmet pressed to helmet, face to face, she made a breathless, tear-filled plea. "Donny. Please, Donny. Let me go."

She drew a long, easy breath.

Now it was Donny who gasped for air. Baris was puzzled but wasted no time to exploit the opportunity. She freed her arms to pound on Donny's head. He desperately tried to detain her and prevent her escape with every last bit of his failing strength. His grip loosened. Baris held Donny's knowing gaze as he took a final breath, and his pupils dilated.

Baris pried herself free of Donny's embrace and floated on toward the crew module. She was jerked backward. "God, no," Baris turned, defeated. She was tethered to Donny. A thick cord led from his backpack to her suit. Together they floated like unborn twins. Donny had unplugged the life support cord from his own backpack and attached it to hers.

Baris squeezed the cord with both hands, awed and ashamed. She recalled how, only a few years earlier, she had brilliantly sold Ladonscorp executives on a project that would save them money and their reputation with investors. But she had never fully convinced herself. She had traded Donny's life for a team of her own and a sense of stability. So who had rescued whom? Tethered to Donny's lifeless body, she could no longer rationalize that what she had done was best for him. Donny was dead. She trained him in obedience. He showed her unconditional love. In seconds, Baris wept for a lifetime.

She wiped the tears of fear and mistrust from her eyes and cheeks against the Valsalva sponge inside her helmet and swapped out her backpack with Donny's. She reached for the closed hatch to the Joshua 10 crew module and discovered her comm switch was off. She flipped it back on.

". . . *not* open the hatch door to the crew module," blared a voice inside her helmet." "Do *not* open the hatch door to the crew module."

Baris rubbed away a thin layer of frost from the hatch window of the crew module. It was as dark as a tomb inside. "Roger that, Houston. Please advise."

"Baris, this is Henry. There was an unresolved coupling error. If you open the hatch, you and Joshua 10 will both leave the station — separately." Henry paused, and Baris could hear him clear his throat. She assumed Henry must have already known that Andy had been trapped inside. "You can thank the engineers who identified the problem in time to warn you. Over."

Baris looked wistfully upon Donny. *Thank you.* Twice he had saved her.

"We do have a different problem," added Henry. "Without the crew module, there's no way to get you from the station to the *Kharon.*"

Baris ran Boyd's decision cycle: observe, orient, decide, "Henry, what about the cargo ship, *Progress*? Rig it to reach the *Kharon.*"

Henry barked at his team. "Can we do that?"

"Dr. Baris is right. Tell her we can probably program it."

"Baris, proceed immediately to the cargo ship," said Henry. "The forward cargo module is pressurized."

"Roger that, Houston." Baris solemnly placed her hand upon the crew module hatch. "We're not all going home."

Baris entered *Progress* and passed through to the cargo module. She was amazed by what she found inside. Andy and Ted floated together unconscious, rolled up inside layers of insulation, crowded by hydroponic plants illuminated by hundreds of orange glow sticks. Baris allowed herself a small smile.

The CapCom beeped in. "Four-hundred meters to intercept." Baris hurried to secure Andy and Ted with cargo cables and tie-downs.

Mission control followed the *Progress* cargo ship's approach to the *Kharon* on live video that streamed from the spaceplane. "Executing roll maneuver to align with the docking target," reported the CapCom. *Progress* twisted across the Mission Control wall screen as it maneuvered toward the *Kharon*.

"*Progress* is not aligned with *Kharon*'s docking port," reported a flight controller.

"How far is she off?" Henry squinted at the screen. "It looks about two meters."

"One point seven five," confirmed an engineer.

Henry directed the team, "We need a manual assist or *Progress* is going to clip *Kharon*'s wings." Then to Baris, "*Progress*, do you copy?"

Baris floated in the cargo module. "Copy."

"Baris, we're going to need you to assist the docking system manually. The program has you off target."

Baris peered out the forward docking hatch. She suddenly became aware of her ship's spinning motion relative to the *Kharon*.

"Locate the touchscreen display on the forward docking hatch."

Baris located the touchscreen. "Got it."

"As soon as *Kharon*'s docking port becomes visible, you will need to activate the screen and select specific items."

Baris touched the blank screen. Nothing happened. "Henry, the screen is blank."

"It can only be activated when you're within range. *Kharon*'s port is a gold funnel surrounded by a gray ring."

"Copy that." Baris returned to the window.

"Heads up, Baris. The port should be visible soon."

Baris looked for the docking port. *Progress* continued to roll as it maneuvered toward the *Kharon*. She became disoriented by the relative motion of the two ships.

"You should see the port."

Baris felt her head spinning, and her vision became hazy. She barely picked out the gray ring in *Kharon*'s blurred image. "I . . . see it." She pressed the touchscreen, and it lit up in Cyrillic letters.

"Okay, Baris, select the green icon, then select item number one and then item number three — in that order."

The colors mixed and blurred across the screen. Baris slipped toward unconsciousness, and she fought to gain control of her senses.

"You only have a few seconds, Baris. In order: green icon, item one, item three."

Baris breathed deeply and surrendered control. She rapidly tapped her selections on the screen. A diagram flashed, which showed the correct alignment of the docking probe and port.

"Done here, Houston."

⟡⟡⟡

Baris and Ted sat comfortably as accidental space tourists aboard the spaceplane *Kharon*. Andy returned from the galley and offered Baris a coffee. "Thank you for saving my life." And considering Baris's slight build, he added, "You're stronger than you look." Baris simply smiled, too exhausted to explain.

The plane began to shudder, and Andy anxiously sat and gripped the armrests. Baris peacefully reclined and closed her eyes.

"In just a few days," the pilot announced, "we will begin our descent into . . ."

⟡⟡⟡

Outside in the silent vacuum of space, a section of the *Kharon* broke off, transformed into a small spacecraft emblazoned with the name, *Friar Laurence,* and secretly sailed away.

Twenty-nine

MOMENTS AFTER THEY LANDED, Andy and Baris were separated and swarmed by medical personnel. Baris was partially reclined in a chair beside the medical trailer. She was roped off from a crowd of onlookers and the press who jockeyed for the best position to snap a picture.

A nurse snuck in close behind Baris. "Dr. Baris, my name is Sarah. Gideon is going to perform some quick tests on your eye pressure." Before Baris could get a look at Gideon, he placed two drops in each of her eyes, stabilized her head with his meaty hands, and tested the surface of each eye. "Limited intracranial hypertension," said Gideon in a deep bass.

While Baris was distracted by the eye tests, Sarah's slender hands glided over the surface of Baris's body exploring every inch of her, even beneath her suit. "Any breaks in your skin? Exposure to blood in your last twenty-four hours aboard the cis —" Henry worked his way through the crowd toward Baris, and Sarah withdrew her hands. She whispered in Baris's ear. "You're not alone, Dr. Baris."

"Not alone?" asked Baris. "Who . . .?" She turned and glimpsed a lissome woman and brawny man disappear among the throng of people.

"Dr. Baris. Henry Laughton." Henry offered Baris an outstretched hand. Before they connected, a ringtone played "Hail to the Chief," and Henry pressed a satellite phone into her palm. "You're gonna want to take that call."

"Hello?" Baris answered.

"Please hold for the President of the United States."

Baris met Tom's eyes through the crowd. He looked uncertain. She dropped the phone on the chair and moved to him. As they embraced, tiny arms wrapped tightly around Baris's legs. Together, they scooped up Amanda into their arms for a mighty hug.

Up the nape of Baris's neck, indigo stripes, like passing clouds, traveled across her skin and disappeared beneath her hair.

ↁ⊲Ⅱↁ⊲Ⅱ

Typheus brooded behind his desk and glared at the giant wall-screen image of the cislunar space station in orbit above the Moon. Daniels whimpered an apology, "I'm told we can recover the body of the chimp."

"Forget the animal," snapped Typheus. "Get me that device."

Thirty

CLICK CLICK. Andy ignited the grill with a *woosh* beneath a beautiful, sunny sky. Balloons that read "Happy Birthday Amanda" decorated the back yard of Baris's home. Baris leaned on Tom, one hand draped over his shoulder; the other rubbed her new baby bump. Bud walked over to Baris with Lou in tow.

"Dr. Baris," said Bud.

"Jessica, please."

"Thank you so much for inviting us."

Lou popped in. "Your daughter . . ." He searched for a name as he pointed to Amanda, who sat in the grass amid a mess of children's books and construction paper.

"Amanda," said Baris, noting all the balloons.

"Has grown up so quickly. I remember when she was only, only . . ."

"We've never seen her before," said Bud, as he spied two men in black enter the yard. He recognized one of the men. "Excuse us, Jessica." Bud elbowed Lou. Lou grinned sheepishly at Baris and followed Bud across the yard to greet Jack Wryder.

"Jess," asked Tom, "who are those guys?"

Baris locked eyes with Jack Wryder and the baby stirred in her womb. "I don't know," she said, as a tingle sizzled up her spine to end as a soft buzz in her ear. "Must be friends of Bud and Lou."

Baris's party had broken up. Bud reclined unconscious on the lawn with a cocktail umbrella in his hair, and Lou flopped beside him into the pile of Amanda's books. A cover with a chubby caterpillar-like creature caught Lou's eye. The title read: "Tardigrades: Nature's Toughest Animals."

"Hey, Bud." Lou yawned. "Wasn't Donny injected with tardigrade something or other?" He opened the book and lazily read aloud. "Tardigrades, also called water bears, can live for years without . . ." Lou drifted off to sleep.

. . . *without food or water, survive in outer space without oxygen and were even brought back to life after being frozen for over thirty years.*

END OF BOOK ONE

"Joshua prayed to the LORD: 'Make the sun stop in the sky . . . and the moon stand still.' So the sun stood still, and the moon stopped."

—Joshua 10

About The Author

JOHN ELGAN changed from a career in big pharma to teach science to high school and college students. He has used storytelling to activate his students' imagination, deep thinking, and emotions to help them make meaningful connections in life beyond the classroom. John is also the author of short stories, four of which are published in *Yellow Diamond: Cautionary Tales of Science Fiction & Fantasy.*

You can find book discussion questions and sign up for updates at johnelgan.com